Stories by Contemporary Writers from Shanghai

THE MOST BEAUTIFUL FACE IN THE WORLD

T0097920

Text: Xue Shu
Translation: Yawtsong Lee
Cover Image: Getty Images
Interior Design: Xue Wenqing
Cover Design: Wang Wei

Copy Editor: Kirstin Mattson
Assistant Editor: Wu Yuezhou
Editorial Director: Zhang Yicong

Senior Consultants: Sun Yong, Wu Ying, Yang Xinci
Managing Director and Publisher: Wang Youbu

ISBN: 978-1-60220-236-8

Address any comments about *The Most Beautiful Face in the World* to:
Better Link Press
99 Park Ave
New York, NY 10016
USA

or

Shanghai Press and Publishing Development Company
F 7 Donghu Road, Shanghai, China (200031)
Email: comments_betterlinkpress@hotmail.com

Printed in China by Shanghai Donnelley Printing Co., Ltd.
1   3   5   7   9   10   8   6   4   2

Two Novellas

THE MOST BEAUTIFUL FACE IN THE WORLD

By Xue Shu

Better Link Press

Foreword

English readers will be presented with a set of pocket books. These books contain outstanding novellas written by writers from Shanghai over the past 30 years. Most of the writers were born in Shanghai after the late 1940's. They started their literary careers during or after the 1980's. For various reasons, most of them lived and worked in the lowest social strata in other cities or in rural areas for much of their adult lives. As a result they saw much of the world and learned lessons from real life before finally returning to Shanghai. They embarked on their literary careers for various reasons, but most of them were simply passionate about writing. The writers are involved in a variety of occupations, including university professors, literary editors, leaders of literary institutions and professional writers. The diversity of topics covered in these novellas will lead readers to discover the different experiences and motivations of the authors. Readers will encounter a fascinating range of esthetic convictions as they analyze the authors' distinctive artistic skills and writing styles. Generally speaking, a realistic writing style dominates most of their literary works. The literary works they have elaborately created are a true reflection of drastic social changes, as well as differing perspectives towards urban life in Shanghai. Some works created by avant-garde writers have been selected in order to present a variety of styles. No matter what writing styles they adopt though, these writers have enjoyed a definite place, and exerted a positive influence, in Chinese literary circles over the past 3 decades.

Known as the "Paris of the Orient" around the world, Shanghai was already an international metropolis in the 1920's and 1930's. During that period, Shanghai was China's economic, cultural and literary center. A high number of famous Chinese writers lived, created and published their literary works in Shanghai, including, Lu Xun, Guo

Moruo, Mao Dun and Ba Jin. Today, Shanghai has become a globalized metropolis. Writers who have pursued a literary career in the past 30 years are now faced with new challenges and opportunities. I am confident that some of them will produce other fine and influential literary works in the future. I want to make it clear that this set of pocketbooks does not include all representative Shanghai writers. When the time is ripe, we will introduce more representative writers to readers in the English-speaking world.

Wang Jiren
Series Editor

Contents

The Most Beautiful Face
in the World

I   Ah-Xing

As his foot cleared the threshold, his body slammed hard into the left door jamb. Ah-Xing felt an instant burning sensation in his shoulder. His immediate reaction was to stop and steady himself. Standing outside the door, he took three deep breaths and lightly flicked his shoulder to remove any dust or whitewash that might have rubbed off on it, before resuming his daily walk to work.

The burning in his shoulder, the momentary sensation of pain transmitted to the brain, seemed reluctant to go away as he continued on toward the massage center called *Xindeng*, or "Heart Light," a term popular with meditative Buddhists. Ah-Xing put up a hand to feel the bulging muscles of his left shoulder and a warm feeling arose inside of him. But no sooner had it started than he checked himself with the sobering words: "Don't let it go to your head, don't be smug, don't forget yourself..."

The series of "don'ts" served as a damper on his uncharacteristic euphoric mood. Ah-Xing was a low-key person and had a realistic sense of his self-worth, his limitations and his station. His run-in with the door jamb raised an immediate red flag in his mind. Such an accident was without precedent. How could he have bumped into the frame of a door through which he had passed countless times without incident for close to thirty years? Imagine a tailor with thirty years of experience under his belt suddenly committing the egregious error of placing the buttonholes on the wrong side of a man's garment one day!

Ah-Xing drew a deep breath and pulled himself together. He was now going to work. Ever conscientious, Ah-Xing believed that nothing was more important than going to work at this moment.

It was nine in the morning, well past the normal rush hour for most people commuting to work or going to school. Only a few straggling bicycles were on the streets, mostly rickety ones that could dispense with a bell because the squeaking of their rusty pedals gave ample warning of their approach. Occasionally a low, hoarse honking could be heard, like a normal voice turned into a feeble plaint when muffled by a multilayered mask. It came from an electric three-wheeled motorbike driven by some disabled person looking to pick up a fare.

Retired women of a mature age sat by the street outside their homes, sorting the vegetables they'd hauled from either the supermarket or the neighborhood vendors that set out their wares only in the morning. On the luffa gourds, the metal peelers made a crisp sound of *sah lah lah, sah lah lah* that seemed to advertise the fact they had been freshly picked that very morning and had gone straight to the market, still firm and juicy. As the green soy beans, called *maodou*, were freed from their pods and thrown into enamel basins, they bounced with a singsong patter like a wild bunch of tap-dancing youths—no sooner had the first four or five beans stopped stamping their feet than another four or five chimed in with their fancy footwork.

The retired men, grandfatherly and avuncular, liked to sit outside their buildings, drinking tea and flicking through newspapers. Blowing through puckered lips, they ruffled the surface of the tea, which then went into their mouths with a fricative sound. Instead of gulping it down, as when they needed to slake an urgent thirst, they savored the scent and sound of the brew that they swirled in their mouths and over their tongues. As they turned the pages of their newspapers, the breeze created a rustle by which you could tell apart the larger-format *Liberation Daily* and the smaller *Xin Min Evening News*.

In this manner Ah-Xing had walked to his workplace day, in day out through the years, rarely departing from routine, through the diminished street noise that followed the din of the morning hustle and bustle. He treaded the narrow, one-foot-wide special path for the blind embedded in the sidewalk. Paved with green tiles bearing raised geometric patterns, it enlivened the three-meter wide, drab-hued sidewalk. Of course Ah-Xing wouldn't know that the path under his feet was green. All he knew was that he had already counted with his feet one hundred and fifty square tiles, and would be at the front door of the massage center after counting another one hundred thirty round tiles.

On this day however, after one hundred fifty square tiles, his feet were surprised by a tile with a herringbone pattern. He ran the soles of his shoes over the raised pattern, rubbing and probing, and came to the conclusion that the tile, which had been broken for many days, had finally been replaced with a new one, probably by the neighborhood committee. But why didn't they replace it with one of the same pattern as before? This new pattern felt funny under his feet.

Once inside the Heart Light Massage Center, Ah-Xing changed into his white coat and walked into Room 03, which was his massage station. Ah-Mei, his assistant, came in a step behind him, and Ah-Xing remarked: "The one hundred fifty-first tile of the blind path has been replaced."

"How can you tell?"

"I have to know. I take that path every single day and it has become part of me."

"Well, I work by your side every single day. Do you know what I'm wearing today?"

With a twitch of his mouth and after rolling his eyes skyward three times, Ah-Xing replied: "You are wearing a suit today, with a skirt, and a fitted blouse."

Ah-Mei said with a giggle: "That's right, Ah-Xing! I'm wearing a bright red skirt suit. It's all the rage this year. It's uncanny; it's as if you could see."

Pointing at his chest, Ah-Xing said: "But I can see! I have an eye in here."

Ah-Mei was not totally blind. She had had normal eyesight when she was little. She even had the prized double eyelids—the type of wider lid with a crease thought desirable by many—and her plum-like dark eyes danced when she looked at you.

One New Year's Day when she was in her early teens, some boy in the neighborhood lit an illegal firework, causing sparks to fall on Ah-Mei's home. When the firefighters pulled Ah-Mei from the attic where she had been sleeping, the two quilts covering her had been charred. She was lucky to have survived the fire but her face suffered severe burns and her eyes were half blind.

In a sense it was a blessing that her eyesight was nearly gone. Now when she sat down to look into a mirror, all she saw was a blur. Even though her severely burned face looked like a lunar scene pockmarked with craters, or a shriveled orange peel, she had no hang-ups about going out and meeting people because she didn't have a clear visual picture of the disfigurement.

Having put on her white work smock over her bright red skirt suit, Ah-Mei started the routine preparations in Room 03 as Ah-Xing watched her from his chair. Yes, Ah-Xing believed he watched the world around him with a mind's eye. He was now watching Ah-Mei pad back and forth before him, setting things up, laying out blankets, folding up towels, and placing bottles of rubbing oil and all kinds of moisturizing and skin care products on the shelves of the work cart. From time to time Ah-

Xing would surprise her with an observation: "Hey, the protein cream should be on the top shelf and the muscle ointment should be on the second shelf. You've just stacked them on the wrong shelves!"

Ah-Mei would giggle and proceed to switch the two items back to their preordained shelves. And following a clinking of bottles, a smile of satisfaction would appear on Ah-Xing's face.

Ah-Xing's eyes looked no different than normal eyes except that they had never exercised their assigned functions. Fortunately his sharp hearing had more than made up for this deficiency. With the aid of his auditory acuity, he could detect that Ah-Mei had failed to stretch the cotton blanket taut enough over the massage bed or that she had left the lid of the protein cream only partially screwed down, not to mention the difference between Ah-Mei's tight-fitting skirt suit and her loose-fitting casual wear.

But these observations paled before his uncanny ability to tell the weather of the day. Natural phenomena, such as wind, dew and fog, were converted in his brain into auditory and tactile information. Anything that impinged on, rubbed against or interacted with his ears or his skin were codes by which he perceived the world around him, as were movements, the rise and fall and the unseen dynamics of things. On the whole Ah-Xing could be a thousand times more sensitive to things that went on about him than sighted people. For that reason, Ah-Xing, who was born blind, had never found his blindness a handicap.

There was only one problem, and that was whenever colors were mentioned. Ah-Xing had a hard time grasping their meaning. When Ah-Mei said she was wearing a bright red dress, Ah-Xing felt a tug at his heart. Bright red? What could it look like? He combed through his memory and vocabulary for any expression to do with "red." As words such as "fire red," "red sun," and "red and swollen" came to mind, there arose in his ears the faint crackling of burning kindling and an occasional wavelet of heat billowed onto his face.

Once the preparations were over, Ah-Mei sat down to wait for customers. Awaking from his reverie Ah-Xing asked Ah-Mei: "Don't you find it very warm today? I feel so warm that it hurts."

Ah-Mei answered with a laugh: "It is a little warm, but it doesn't hurt me."

Feeling his left shoulder with his hand, Ah-Xing thought to himself: "Well, maybe you don't, but I hurt."

II   Yu Manli

As a blind person with nearly thirty years of practice, Ah-Xing moved about with ease and rarely bumped into people or tripped. So he could probably attribute what happened earlier that day to a special circumstance.

Before leaving home, he'd received a phone call from Granny Yan, the grandmother of the Yan family, who said to him: "Ah-Xing, I already mentioned I wanted to match you up with this Chen jia meimei." Because family was so important, she referred to the girl by her family relationship, daughter of the Chen family, rather than by her given name. Granny Yan continued: "She has agreed to meet you this evening. So put on something decent for the first date. I'll come with you."

After hanging up the phone, Ah-Xing got ready to go to work with the words of Granny Yan still ringing in his ears. It was then that his shoulder had hit the door jamb.

Ah-Xing was considered an educated person, having obtained a diploma from a vocational school upon the completion of a training program for blind masseurs. In his interactions with people, his daily affairs and his demeanor, he was like an old-school gentleman. He kept his back ramrod straight, with his well-shaped head supported on a neck that was neither too long nor too short. He rarely turned his head left or right; occasionally he would tip it sideways, as if listening with a rapt expression on his face. He was a picture of trustworthiness and reliability.

Thus sat Ah-Xing in his chair in the massage room, his head turned slightly so that one ear was oriented toward the front. At just past ten in the morning, he heard the noise of slippers on the concrete floor drawing nearer in the corridor. That told Ah-Xing he had a customer, who had changed into the terrycloth robe and plastic slippers provided by the massage center.

The Heart Light Massage Center, run by the neighborhood collective, was a small outfit containing only three massage rooms and employing three masseurs. Without waiting for the customer to come into the room, Ah-Xing left his chair and made his way toward the door so that by the time the footsteps were at the threshold, Ah-Xing would be exactly one meter from it, saying: "Good morning, miss!"

For by listening to the footsteps Ah-Xing was able to determine the gender of the customer. This customer answered with a distracted, perfunctory "hmm." So it was indeed a woman. She handed the service order to Ah-Mei, who brought it so close to her face to read it that you would think she was trying to sniff out the words with her nose. Then Ah-Mei called out a loud greeting: "Good morning, Miss Yu Manli! You are here today for a back massage. Please lie down on the bed."

With that announcement, Ah-Mei left the room to fetch the hot water for hot towel compresses. Kicking off her plastic slippers, which fell on the floor with a soft thud, this female customer called Yu Manli lay down and stretched herself out on the massage bed. Seated on a high stool at the head of the bed, where he faced the crown of the customer's head, Ah-Xing, his head slightly upturned, asked in a soft voice, calling her by her given name: "Miss Manli, do you have any special requests?"

It was typical of Ah-Xing to be so considerate. Treating his customers like family, he would omit their surname when addressing them, and it was this familiarity that had earned him many a regular customer. But Yu Manli did not take kindly to it at all. Using the term for "master" she replied coolly: "Hey, *shifu*! Please don't call me 'Miss.'"

Ah-Xing immediately apologized: "Oh, I'm sorry. You see, recently a lady of a certain age took offense when I called her 'Elder Sister,' and asked me, 'Do I look that old to you?' So I started calling her 'Miss,' which cheered her up."

The only reaction on the part of Yu Manli, who was in a supine position, was a small explosion of air from her mouth. Ah-Xing read it as a suppressed laugh from the customer. Rubbing his hands together, Ah-Xing said: "Manli, turn over and lie on your stomach. You are getting a back massage to loosen up the *jinluo*, the passages for air or blood, and improve blood circulation along your spine."

Now that Ah-Xing was calling her "Manli," omitting the title of "Miss," Yu Manli found it too familiar and a bit awkward. But the awkwardness was accompanied by an unmistakably warm and pleasant feeling. Yu Manli enjoyed, after all, being called "Manli" in a soft voice by a mature man. Besides, he was a blind man, who couldn't even see her face.

In no time she was able to overcome this awkwardness. She turned over as Ah-Xing directed her face to a hollow lined with dry towels at the head of the bed. The hollow was just large enough for the nose and the mouth, so that she was able to breathe normally even in this face down position. Ah-Mei brought in a basin filled with hot water, which she set down on the cart, and went out, closing the door quietly.

Ah-Xing proceeded to give the customer a hot compress and a back rub. Taking a hot towel out of the boiling water and wringing it dry, Ah-Xing spread it on the back of her neck, and pressed down on it with his palm several times, using only a fraction of his full force. A muffled cry issued from Yu Manli's mouth: "Ouch! It hurts."

Ah-Xing laughed, revealing his white teeth: "I know it hurts, because there's a lot that's wrong with your spine. Massage is a therapy, a treatment. So you'll need to bear with the pain for now. A course of treatment normally consists of eight visits. After eight sessions, the pain will go away, I promise."

As Ah-Xing eased off her terrycloth robe, Yu Manli instantly felt a chill on her bared back, which was now exposed to the cooler surrounding air. Overcoming a momentary attack of modesty, she relaxed, comforted by the thought that a blind man wouldn't be able to see anything. Besides, what was there to see but a bare back?

Ah-Xing's professional ethics were such that he considered work the most important part of his life. Everyday he came into direct contact with the skin, muscles, bones and hair of people from all walks of life. Nothing gave him greater satisfaction than when people were relieved of lumbar and back pains, stiff necks and muscle sprains, returning to good health through the magic touch of his hands.

While his hands, acting as his eyes, could detect gender, age and body mass, and could tell the difference between people engaged in physical labor and those doing office work, they were as pure and ethical as the man owning them. They would work equally conscientiously on the body of a client whether it was that of an attractive young woman or a man with bulging muscles, and they certainly would never overstep the bounds of propriety. The duration of the contact between his hands and the body they worked on would always be just right, in conformity with therapeutic need and the norm of the trade. His was a pair of safe hands, and a masseur owning a pair of safe hands had to be a safe person. Blindness in both eyes certainly bumped up his safety rating a great deal.

The body he was working on today was that of a woman who was not a girl anymore. The moment Ah-Xing's hands came into contact with Yu Manli's neck, he could detect a certain flabbiness and knottiness. The flab was a natural result of the ageing of muscles and skin past their prime. The knots were from the swelling and twisting of what traditional Chinese medicine referred to as the *jinmai* passages along the cervical vertebrae; caused by prolonged strain, it was not normally as severe in the neck of a younger woman.

As Ah-Xing rubbed her back parallel to the grain of her muscles, Yu Manli breathed in, making hissing sounds. These were partly moans of pain and partly expressions of relief. It was as if torrents of toxins were released from her body as her shoulders and back warmed up under the kneading and rubbing of Ah-Xing's hands.

After an hour and half, the back rub was done. Ah-Xing said with a light pat on her bared shoulder: "You're done, Manli. Walk around and see if you feel loosened up."

Pulling her bathrobe back around her, Yu Manli got off the bed, stepped into the plastic slippers and took a few steps, turning her neck a few times. She did indeed feel much better. Planting herself in front of the mirror in the corner, she tidied up her hair, which had been mussed when she lay on the cot. Then she pulled the front of her robe to one side and touched her shoulder, saying: "Hey, my shoulder is all red from your rubbing. No wonder it hurts here."

At these words, Ah-Xing, who was putting things in order on the cart with his head slightly turned sideways, said in the general direction of the mirror: "Red? And it hurts still? I may have used greater force given the severity of your neck problems. I apologize."

Closing the front opening of her bathrobe, Yu Manli replied: "I like when it hurts a little."

When she said she liked it, the tone was icy.

Yu Manli went out of the room in her slippers. Ah-Xing, cocking his head, listened for the sound of the slippers, which grew fainter until it disappeared altogether. He sat by the massage bed musing: "Women like red dresses. Do they all like the sensation of a little pain?"

Ah-Mei walked in on his reverie and said with a mysterious air: "Ah-Xing, according to Xiao Lin, this Yu Manli is really ugly, so indescribably ugly that she looks like Peking Man."

Xiao Lin, the cashier at the center's main counter, was the only seeing employee. Ah-Mei went on: "I saw a picture of Peking Man when I was little. It had protruding teeth and a jaw that thrust out. It was on the lower rungs of evolution and resembled a great ape. Have you ever seen an ape?"

She checked herself. Talking about the little she retained from her childhood visual memory, and what little she could see now with her impaired sight, could been seen as flaunting knowledge that Ah-Xing might consider an unattainable luxury.

However, she abandoned the topic not out of a concern for Ah-Xing's feelings but because she ran out of words with which to describe Peking Man and the great apes.

But it got Ah-Xing thinking: "I just did a back rub for Yu Manli, so I didn't get to feel her face. Peking Man? Is Peking Man really that ugly?"

III   Chen Jia Meimei

In the course of the day Ah-Xing worked on five customers. Yu Manli was the only woman. This was the norm; eighty percent of the center's customers were men. At about four in the afternoon Ah-Xing asked the manager to give him the evening off. This meant he would forgo a substantial amount of earnings, because there were more customers in the evening than during the daytime. But tonight was the first date with Chen jia meimei—the daughter of the Chen family—that Granny Yan had arranged. She had told him: "Chen jia meimei looked at your picture and liked what she saw."

Ah-Xing had given Granny Yan a two-inch passport photo taken when he was hired by the massage center, the same one used on the pass that he now wore everyday to work. Ah-Xing had no idea how engaging he looked in that photo. But since Chen jia meimei liked it, he liked it too.

Ah-Xing was in no mood to cook a decent supper for himself. He poured some boiling water into a bowl of cold rice left over from the day before, added pieces of pickled cucumber, and slurped it up in record time. He then immediately started to get dressed for the date. There was a wool sweater his elder brother and sister-in-law had given him for his birthday. His sister-in-law said on the occasion: "Ah-Xing, this is an open-neck sweater, a famous brand, and it's ash gray, a very tasteful color."

When Ah-Xing accepted the gift from his sister-in-law, her hand did not release it quickly enough, and Ah-Xing came into contact with her warm, fleshy palm. Opening the cellophane wrapping, Ah-Xing felt the wool sweater with his hand and asked:

"What does ash gray look like?"

His brother said: "Well, ash gray is the color of cigarette ash. Do you know what cigarette ash is? Its color..."

After spending quite some time trying to explain it, his brother found he was unable to adequately describe the color of ash gray. So he took an easy way out: "Anyway, you can feel it with your hand. Whatever you feel will be the color of ash gray."

So Ah-Xing passed his hand all over the sweater and picked up a corner with two fingers, lightly rubbing it between them. Then he knew what the color of ash gray was. It was a warm, soft, fluffy color. What was it like? Ah-Xing found a sensation that could be a surrogate for the color; he decided that ash gray was the warm, fleshy palm of his sister-in-law. His sister-in-law was a warm, fleshy ball herself. She was not exactly fat but was what the locals of Shanghai would describe as *xiao jiegun*, meaning small in build but firm of flesh and round in shape. At the time she married into their family, Ah-Xing was only fourteen. When she was in the mood, she would sometimes rub his head or put an arm around his shoulder. It was then that Ah-Xing found out his sister-in-law was a certifiable *xiao jiegun*.

Since Ah-Xing never saw colors, they were interpreted in his brain as a temperature, a sound or a smell. To Ah-Xing's mind, bright red was Ah-Mei and ash gray was his sister-in-law.

Ah-Xing put on the sweater, beneath which he wore a white shirt. His dress slacks were crisp and unwrinkled except for a clear crease across both trouser legs at knee height, apparently the result of being folded and kept in a chest drawer for a long time. Of course those creases were unimportant, for Ah-Xing now looked very smart and presentable. That's what counted.

When Granny Yan came for him, she couldn't help exclaiming in wonder: "Ah-Xing, you would rate a ten in good looks if it were not for your blindness!" Since she was a neighbor who had seen Ah-Xing grow up from a tot, Ah-Xing never minded her mention of his blindness.

It was getting dark as Ah-Xing, chaperoned

by Granny Yan, went on this first date. The agreed place was the recreation room of the neighborhood committee, not far from his home. The room was divided in two; the outer area, equipped with four or five square tables, was the venue for senior citizens' after-dinner activities. The jingling sound of tiles being shuffled for a new game arose from the tables where mahjongg was being played. The lively shouts of *chi*, *peng* or *hula*, uttered by the players when they drew a tile or completed a certain move, had a hoarse quality characteristic of older adults but that didn't mean they were any less excitable than younger people.

At two other tables, poker was being played. Players sorted and flicked their cards, spreading them out in a fan shape before returning them to a neat pile, which was tapped noisily against the table. Some played their hand in a highly emotional state, slapping down their cards as if they were weapons trotted out in a show of force, the sound reminiscent of the shooting of a BB gun.

Against this noisy background one could also

hear the sounds of Chinese chess pieces hitting the wooden board, advancing with hesitation, retreating, going after the opponent in hot pursuit or making a flanking maneuver. These sounds, compared to those of mahjongg and poker, were tamer and more deliberate. In this world where the elderly were unperturbed by the younger generation, they experienced a second childhood, shedding all pretenses of dignified deportment and playing with abandon, just like children unsupervised by adults. All their illnesses, pains and frailties, as well as their patriarchal authority, were thrown to the wind in this playful frenzy.

They arrived a little early, so Ah-Xing "watched" the games played by the aunties and uncles in the outer room for a while before Granny Yan whispered into his ear: "She's here. She's here."

With that, Granny Yan drew him into the inner room, which was a small reading room lined with simple shelves stacked with all sorts of magazines, including *Health*, *Family* and *TV Guide Weekly*. To accommodate Ah-Xing, the neighborhood committee had asked the readers to leave for the evening.

No sooner had Granny Yan sat Ah-Xing in a chair than the sound of the footsteps of two people could be heard at the door. A woman whose voice he did not recognize exchanged brief greetings with Granny Yan, from which he gleaned the information that the woman was Chen jia muma, the mother of the Chen family. And Chen jia muma was heard to say: "Oh, so this is Ah-Xing!"

Ah-Xing got up from his chair and nodded his head in the direction of the voice. Then after some consideration, he turned toward a spot to the immediate right of Chen jia muma, where a soft, rustling sound was being made, and nodded a second time. The second bow was his greeting to the daughter, Chen jia meimei. The greetings out of the way, Chen jia muma said with a hearty laugh: "Sit down, Ah-Xing. Sit down."

This was followed by the voice of Granny Yan: "Chen jia meimei, this is Ah-Xing. You've seen his photograph."

A slight flush rose in Ah-Xing's face and a smile gathered on his mouth. It would have been a winning smile except that it was accompanied by a rolling of his eyes with the lamp light glinting off the whites, giving a false impression of slyness to the smile and spoiling it.

All he could hear from the girl called Chen jia meimei was some more of the same rustling sound but no words. Probably she was wearing a brand new dress and she was a little uncomfortable at this arranged meeting with a potential marriage partner. The rustling must have come from the squirming of a tense body in a stiff new dress.

Then Granny Yan and Chen jia muma started their conversation, with Granny Yan reeling off Ah-Xing's family and professional background, personal qualities and temperament, and Chen jia muma singing the praises of her daughter, who was artless, vivacious, kind and blessed with good sense.

Ah-Xing, his head slightly inclined, was all ears. Chen jia meimei also remained silent and did not participate in the conversation. The dialogue between the two elderly women went on for nearly twenty minutes before it abruptly broke off, as if they realized that to go on would inevitably lead to a disclosure of all their family secrets. An awkward silence descended after three discreet coughs from Chen jia muma followed by Granny Yan's equally dry chuckle. The noises from the mahjongg and poker games in the next room suddenly sounded louder in the silence.

The awkward silence was broken by Chen jia meimei, who spoke up unexpectedly. She was addressing Ah-Xing: "Hey, do you know Andy Lau?"

This was a child's voice, bell-like, crisp and clear, belonging to a girl whose body was still developing. Ah-Xing was caught off guard by this sudden high note that interrupted the silent interval. Sensing the question was addressed to him, he hastened to say: "Andy Lau? Oh, I don't know him but I do know about him. He's a popular singer from Hong Kong."

Chen jia meimei was instantly transformed into a bird. He heard the sound of a stool being moved followed by the pitter patter of footsteps on the floor. The bird flew to Ah-Xing's side, chirping: "I know Andy Lau. He came to our home. I had told him to come at six in the afternoon but he came early, just when I was taking a bath. Andy Lau said, 'Open up, let me in.' I said, 'Wait a sec, just a second, I am in the middle of taking a bath...'"

Ah-Xing was astonished by the intimacy between Chen jia meimei and Andy Lau. On the other hand, maybe this Andy Lau was not the same as the Hong Kong pop singer, but a friend or relative of the Chen family who happened to have the same name. But when Chen jia meimei continued her account, Ah-Xing no longer knew what to think. She went on ebulliently: "Andy Lau said, 'I will be performing in a concert this evening, on a big stage. I will not be able to wait until you finish your bath. Just go to my concert. I'll leave a ticket for you in the letter box.' Oh, by the way, have you ever seen Andy Lau in a concert?"

Ah-Xing gave an unenthusiastic answer: "No."

Chen jia meimei glowed with pride: "I went to one of his concerts. Andy Lau gave me a ticket for the first row."

Chen jia muma interrupted her daughter: "Meimei, it's time we go home."

But there was no stopping Chen jia meimei, who was just warming to the subject: "Andy Lau said, 'Make sure you come this evening.' Then he left, because he was so busy. He had a concert to prepare for."

Granny Yan tried to steer her away from the subject: "Meimei, this dress you are wearing looks so pretty. Where did you buy it? I must get one of these for my granddaughter."

The diversion worked and Chen jia meimei was drawn to the new topic. "Papa took me to the Shanghai No. 1 Department Store and bought it for me. There were so many dresses in the store and I picked four. But papa only let me have one, so I settled on this orange dress. It's pretty, isn't it? Orange is my favorite color. I wore it to Andy Lau's concert. I told Andy Lau, 'I'm taking a bath, wait a sec...'"

Chen jia meimei managed to return again to the topic of Andy Lau. Her rambling monologue was a blur in Ah-Xing's consciousness as he mulled over the color of orange. He was familiar with oranges. They had a round shape and were cool to the touch. You remove the peel and eat the segments inside, which are sweet and tart and juicy. Now, the color of orange was no longer just cool, sweet, tart and juicy to Ah-Xing, it was also something else, but what was it? As the name of Andy Lau kept popping up in Chen jia meimei's continuing narrative in the background, it suddenly struck him that the color of orange must be a color of passion, a passion bordering on madness that had no regard for occasion or propriety, and caused people to talk to themselves. This Chen jia meimei was an orange and must have a round face shaped like an orange. It was only natural she would wear the color of oranges.

Chen jia muma was finally able to persuade a reluctant Chen jia meimei to leave with her. As they went out of the door, she was still singing: "Oh, give me a cup of nepenthe, to keep me dry-eyed at night. Give me a cup of nepenthe, to banish sorrow from my life…"

Her clear voice with its child-like quality trailed off as mother and daughter disappeared along the corridor outside the office of the neighborhood committee. Ah-Xing heard the aunties and uncles in the game room burst into peals of laughter.

IV   A Horse-Head Fiddle

That night Ah-Xing tossed and turned in his bed. He kept his eyes closed but sleep eluded him. Keeping his eyes shut really made no difference; all the cacophony and tumult, the temptations and demons of the world, were rooted in his mind. Insomnia is especially hard to bear for the blind.

One question kept sleep at bay: is a blind person fated to settle for someone missing a limb or a mind as a wife? He had never considered his blindness a disability or a deficiency. He believed that his perception and quickness of response were even superior to those of some seeing people. His ears and skin were his eyes.

But all the potential marriage partners fixed up for him by friends and family had one deficiency or another. They also believed that a blind wife for a blind man was a no-no. How was she going to take care of him if they both were blind? But Ah-Xing didn't think he needed others to take care of him. His parents cared for him until he was eight, when they died. His elder brother took care of him until he was fourteen, when his brother got married. Ever since then he had been taking care of himself.

Chen jia meimei was the third date arranged for him. The first was a deaf person, who could not hear a word of what he said in the meeting. To his mind, ears were vital. How could Ah-Xing stand living for the rest of his life with someone who had lost the use of their ears?

The second date suffered from polio. According to the matchmaker, she had some degree of atrophy from her waist down, and her legs were crooked, but it wouldn't affect her everyday functions or her ability to give birth. In the end it was the polio-impaired woman who found him wanting, saying she could accept a deaf or mute person but never a blind person for a husband. Why? A blind person would not be able to see her pretty face, that's why. Ah-Xing found that laughable, for if he could see her pretty face, he could also see her ugly crooked legs.

Granny Yan had told him that Chen jia meimei had everything you could hope for in a marriage partner. Admittedly, she could do with a little more sense in her head but she was not retarded, just artless and childlike. To Ah-Xing's mind, nothing was wrong with that. An artless girl would be pure at heart. She wouldn't look down on you simply because you were blind. But nothing prepared him for how "artless" Chen jia meimei turned out to be.

At the age of nine, Chen jia meimei came down with an illness accompanied by symptoms including muscle cramps, fainting spells and prolonged high fever. After she recovered from the illness, everything appeared to be back to normal. She ate and went to school as usual. But while she eventually reached physical maturity, her mental growth stagnated. You wouldn't know it as long as she kept her mouth shut.

But the moment she talked, the childishness of her speech became clear. Her parents took her to the best hospitals in search of a remedy but the verdict was unanimous: the illness to which she had succumbed as a child had effectively stopped her mental growth.

Ah-Xing was in a quandary. Chen jia meimei was indeed not that disabled; she was curious about and receptive to new ideas, information and knowledge of the world around her. She appreciated pretty dresses. She was capable of showing dedication to her idol Andy Lau and her singing was not bad at all. The only incongruence was the childlike fantasies in her head. Adults have dreams and fantasies too; the difference is that children are not ashamed of verbalizing them. Chen jia meimei had a perception of the world reflective of the intellect of a child. But if she was considered to possess the intellect of a nine-year-old, then she was already very smart for a nine-year-old. She was like a precocious child whose innocence would irrepressibly peep out from under the veneer of her imitative adult speech and deportment.

If he were to form a family with a person who had a permanently stunted intellect, it would be tantamount to adopting a daughter. But if a woman afflicted with polio had refused to marry him, what prospects were there for a normal woman to agree to marry a blind man like him?

Of late Ah-Xing had appeared distracted and absent-minded at work. During the lulls when customers were far and few between, he would be seen sitting straight-backed on the stool in his massage room, his posture poised and his mind in quiet commotion.

That day, Ah-Mei asked: "Ah-Xing, are you getting married?"

Ah-Xing was startled out of his reverie. Jerking like a shrimp underwater surprised by an intrusive hand, he asked: "Who told you that? Cut the nonsense!"

Ah-Mei said with a giggle: "It's Chen jia meimei, right? Still trying to keep me in the dark, eh?"

Ah-Xing was quick to clarify: "We met only once. Nothing was decided."

She was not pleased with his attempt at denial. "Chen jia meimei has publicly said that Xu Shixing is her boyfriend," she stated, using Ah-Xing's formal full name. "So don't try to deny it. Not to me."

Ah-Mei considered herself Ah-Xing's close friend, and she also possessed a simple self-confidence that rarely allowed for the possibility of error.

Failing to come up with a convincing explanation, Ah-Xing put up a lame defense: "It's not what you think, not what…"

Feigning annoyance, Ah-Mei responded with a snort and a rolling of her eyes in the direction of Ah-Xing, which was of course wasted on him. He was miffed that after only one meeting with him Chen jia meimei would be so reckless as to publicly announce that he was her boyfriend. He felt deprived of his freedom of choice.

Chatter in the corridor just outside the room meant they had a customer coming. Ah-Xing got off his stool and Ah-Mei went out of the room, abandoning for the moment the subject of Ah-Xing's girlfriend. She soon returned to the room to announce with a mysterious air: "Peking Man is here. She's getting her order written up at the main counter."

With an "oh," Ah-Xing remembered. The customer Ah-Mei dubbed Peking Man was Yu Manli. The sound of slippered feet drew nearer in the corridor. Judging from the tread, the speed and the rhythm, he knew the customer was walking toward Room 03. He made for the door, and just as he was about to reach it, Yu Manli pushed it open. Ah-Mei greeted her and took the work order before leaving the room to fetch hot water. In the meantime Ah-Xing had the customer lie down on the massage bed. He drew a breath before saying: "How are you, Manli? This will be your second back massage…"

Lying face up on the massage bed, Yu Manli interrupted Ah-Xing: "Instead of a back rub, I'd like a head massage today. I have a terrible headache."

Ah-Xing said: "All right. If you have a headache, I would recommend an ear candle following the head massage. The result would be much better."

"Do what you have to do, just make the headache go away." She sounded lackadaisical as if weighed down by a feeling of world-weariness, as if she was so tired and helpless she had lost the strength and the will to make an effort.

Ah-Xing picked up a towel from his work cart, laid one hand confidently on the forehead of Yu Manli and unfurled the towel with a jerk of his other hand. He was able to wrap it expertly and neatly around her head so that all her hair, down to the bangs, disappeared under the towel, leaving her face exposed—the forehead, the nose, the cheeks, the jaws, the chin and the neck.

Ah-Mei brought in the hot water and placed it within easy reach of Ah-Xing's right hand. The timing was perfect and now Ah-Xing was all set to begin his work. Once he entered work mode, Ah-Xing banished all idle thoughts from his mind and became absorbed in the task at hand.

Ah-Xing picked up a hot, wet towel and wrung out some of the water before covering Yu Manli's face with it. Holding her chin with one hand, he carefully wiped her face with the moist towel in his other hand. Applying two drops of rubbing oil to his palms, Ah-Xing proceeded to cover with his palms the face looking up at him. As his hands traced the contours of the face, a picture of it began to form in his mind. Then his hands and his mind exclaimed in a chorus of awe and wonder: "What a face!"

Ah-Xing's hands had come into contact with faces of all shapes and sizes: oval, oblong, square, diamond-shaped, you name it. But Yu Manli's face stood out. He couldn't put it in any of the categories known to him. All the features were in their right places, but each of them was proportionally either too small or too large.

The forehead, as if chiseled with a knife, was too short and shallow, dropping off precipitately from a prominent brow, which resembled the raised earthen wall at either side of a battlefield trench, a jagged ridge. The nose was a low knoll, its wings spread wide. She had a very prominent maxilla and mandible, and her jaw was hard and crooked, as if she had a huge rock clamped between her upper and lower teeth. Her cheek bones were hills set far apart, giving her face the feel of a wide open field. The unusual height of the cheek bones added a quality of loneliness and savageness to the vast open space, an openness that lacked order. All the features were thrown together haphazardly to produce this unfamiliar and intriguing face.

With meticulous care Ah-Xing explored the face; his fingers pressed, kneaded and rubbed it, feeling its rises and hollows and the nuances of its skin temperature. With a deft touch that adapted pressure and rhythm to the terrain of her face, he was able to draw in his mind a detailed topographic map of the face with all its features.

In his mind, he replayed all the faces that he had ever massaged and came to the conclusion that the face of Yu Manli was in a class by itself. To the eyes of seeing people, she had the face of Peking Man or a great ape, but to Ah-Xing, hers was a wonderful face. Why did he find it so wonderful? Ah-Xing thought hard about this. Then he decided that he found it wonderful because had never before come across a face like it.

Ah-Xing's palms and fingers crawled and danced dozens of times across Yu Manli's face. His hands were like a farmer opening up untilled land for cultivation. The farmer came upon this piece of land and started to till it with diligence and loving care. Since he was the discoverer of the land, it was something special and beautiful, and he treasured it all the more for that reason. Every curve, every corner, or every flaw for that matter, of this land would be considered an idiosyncrasy that distinguished it from any other land.

The sloping forehead, the prominent brow, the deep sunken eyes, the broad and flaring nostrils, the hard and angular jawbone—all these features painted in sweeping, broad strokes came together to create something with a musical quality. It was not the soft, sweet sounds characteristic of the string instruments of south China, but...what was it?

He thought for a long while before the *matouqin*, the horse-head fiddle, came to mind. The horse-head fiddle produces a sound that swings wildly between extremes. In the first couple of bars, you might think you were hearing the moaning of blasts of sand or that the fiddle was poorly tuned. But if you kept listening, you would be struck by a beauty that is all its own, that subverts all traditions of melody and rhythm. Yes, no mistake about it! Yu Manli's face was the music that came from a horse-head fiddle!

He blurted out to that face: "Manli, you have a very beautiful face!"

As soon as the words tumbled out of his mouth, Ah-Xing could feel his cheeks burning. His face must be close to crimson now, he thought; it even hurt a little from the burning. Ah-Xing got to his feet and walked to the cupboard in the corner. He didn't really need anything from the cupboard, but he stalled for a while, foraging around and taking out a bottle of night cream before going back to his stool. With calm and a normal temperature now restored to his burning face, Ah-Xing readied his hands to resume the massage.

When his hands came into contact with Yu

Manli's face again, he was surprised by the copious warm wetness covering it.

V   A Kiss on the Check

Yu Manli emerged from the massage room with swollen red eyes. Clearly she had been crying. After she paid and left, Xiao Lin asked Ah-Mei: "Why's Peking Man crying? Did Ah-Xing do something to upset her?"

Ah-Mei didn't know, for there was an unwritten rule in the center discouraging the presence of a third party when a masseur worked on a client. Ah-Mei's task was to set things up for the session and greet the customer; after that she had no business staying in the room. Therefore she wasn't privy to what Ah-Xing did or said to the client during the massage session. If a masseur did something improper, the client could always lodge a complaint, but none had been made by Yu Manli.

Xiao Lin, as the only seeing person in the

called "Warlords." Ah-Xing was not too enthusiastic about it. In the first place, if he went, he would not so much be seeing as hearing the movie. If he was invited to a concert, he would have more incentive to go. Moreover Andy Lau was Chen jia meimei's favorite, not his. He loved music, both classical and modern, but of the pop singers, he liked Zhao Chuan and his song, "I May Be Ugly, But I'm Gentle."

But Granny Yan insisted: "Go, Ah-Xing. To get the tickets she had to wait in a long line. She said there will be some kind of ceremony before the show. The director and the actors will attend."

Ah-Xing guessed this must be a so-called premiere. Maybe Andy Lau would show up today. That was the real reason for Chen jia meimei's interest. He was touched by the fact that she'd thought of buying a ticket for him. It would really disappoint her if he didn't go. So he agreed after some thought. Granny Yan reminded him, using the Shanghai slang for taxi: "Call a *chatou* to go to the cinema. It's easier than taking a bus 'cause Chen jia meimei doesn't know the way and you can't see."

After supper Ah-Xing waited for Chen jia meimei outside the office of the neighborhood committee, clutching the movie ticket in his hand. When she was told they were taking a taxi to the movie theater, she exclaimed with joy in her bell-like voice: "Oh! We are taking a taxi! We are going to a movie! Ah-Xing, I know how to hail a taxi. Let me do it."

Ah-Xing said with a laugh: "Fine. I don't know how to hail one. You do it."

Chen jia meimei said with condescension: "Don't you even know how to hail a taxi? Let me teach you. If you see a red plaque on the windshield that says 'vacant,' it means you can hail it. If the plaque is not there, then it means it has been called by someone else. Understand?"

Ah-Xing nodded his understanding.

Then Chen jia meimei suddenly raised her voice to shout: "Taxi, taxi!"

A sharp screech of car brakes told Ah-Xing that the cab had pulled up in front of them. Chen jia meimei darted in like a mouse, leaving Ah-Xing to fend for himself. But Ah-Xing had no difficulty at all getting into the taxi. Inside, Chen jia meimei retold the story of her famous "date" with Andy Lau, causing the driver to cast numerous glances at her in the rearview mirror. Ah-Xing was embarrassed. Going out with someone who was physically grown-up but had the intellect of a child was not something to be proud of. But he couldn't very well cover her mouth with his hand, so he muzzled himself instead and kept silent throughout the taxi ride.

They sat in a pitch dark theater at the multiplex until show time, when they learned it was not an actual premiere but a publicity stunt of the cinema, attended by a few minor actors in the movie and supplemented by local celebrities. One singer gave a good performance mimicking one of Andy Lau's songs. He sounded so much like Andy that Chen jia meimei almost swore it was the man himself. Clutching Ah-Xing's arm and shaking it insistently, she asked with excitement in her voice: "Is he Andy Lau? Is he?"

Ah-Xing overheard a comment by someone who sat nearby: "He's so fat. He'd be more convincing as that chubby singer Liu Huan."

The promotional event lasted about half an hour. When the movie started, Chen jia meimei quieted down, probably because the real Andy Lau finally showed his face—on screen. But after barely ten minutes she was no longer able to keep still. She told Ah-Xing she wanted ice cream. Ah-Xing took her to the snack bar and bought her a Menglong brand ice cream bar, which she started eating as they walked back to their seats. No sooner did they sit down than the ice cream was finished, and Chen jia meimei started squirming in her seat again. She said: "I saw popcorn when we went to get ice cream." So Ah-Xing took her out to get the popcorn. The moviegoers in their row had now stood up twice to let them pass. Ah-Xing heard someone say: "All these comings and goings! They're really busy!"

After buying the popcorn, Ah-Xing didn't want to go back in. He suggested to Chen jia meimei: "Andy Lau will not show up tonight. Let's go home."

Chen jia meimei showed the utmost reluctance: "My mom says it's a shameful waste to throw things away when they are still useable. It's also a waste not to watch a movie to the end after paying good money for the tickets."

Ah-Xing retorted: "So if a patient pays for a bottle of medicine and gets well after taking half of it, does he have to finish the rest of the bottle?"

As Chen jia meimei struggled for an answer Ah-Xing changed the subject by saying: "Let's go. We'll take a taxi back, and I'll buy you mutton shish kebabs."

With a joyous cheer, she agreed to leave immediately.

Ah-Xing brought Chen jia meimei back to their apartment block, at the gate of which a vendor sold barbecued mutton from morning till midnight. Ah-Xing bought ten sticks. As she attacked the shish kebabs with relish, Chen jia meimei said: "Ah-Xing, I need to go home now. Mom is waiting for me."

Ah-Xing said: "I'll see you home. I can't let you walk home alone this late at night."

Chen jia meimei raised no objection and walked on, all the while munching on the kebabs.

Walking at her side, Ah-Xing said abruptly: "Stop telling everybody that Xu Shixing is your boyfriend."

"Why?" Her speech was garbled due to the mouthful of kebabs.

"No reason. It's just not good to broadcast it."

Chen jia meimei cackled with laughter. "I know why. You're shy. Fine, if anyone asks me again, I'll tell them Xu Shixing is not my boyfriend."

Ah-Xing didn't know whether to laugh or cry, but he gave up trying to make her understand. She then said: "Ah-Xing, don't tell my mom you bought me ice cream, popcorn and shish kebabs. She doesn't want me to accept food from others. If she finds out, I'm going to get an earful."

Ah-Xing promised: "I won't tell her."

Chen jia meimei was touched. "Ah-Xing, you're so nice to me. You bought me Menglong ice cream, which costs five yuan! My mom only buys me Yili ice cream for one fifty. You bought me popcorn. My mom says if I eat greasy food right after a cold snack, I will get a bellyache. But I know she says that because she doesn't want to spend the money to get those snacks for me. Mom also tells me not to eat anything from a street vendor. If she finds out you bought shish kebabs for me, you'll get a scolding too. Ah-Xing, you're so nice to me. You'll buy me snacks again, won't you?"

As she droned on, Ah-Xing thought to himself: "This is the first time, and probably the last time, I treat you to a snack."

Chen jia meimei continued: "Ah-Xing, in TV shows, when a boy and a girl date, they kiss each other's cheek. My mom told me to be nice to you on the date. Do we kiss each other's cheek?"

Ah-Xing was startled by the question. "What? Kiss each other's cheek? That's not necessary."

Chen jia meimei came to a halt. "Ah-Xing, this is where I live. I'm going in now. Since people on a date are supposed to kiss each other goodbye, they do on television, let's kiss."

Without waiting for an answer, she threw her arms around Ah-Xing's neck. Before he could push her away, he felt a greasy, warm and mutton-smelling mouth come into contact with his cheek, and heard a loud "pop" when the lips gave his face a big smack. Then Chen jia meimei let go, saying cheerily: "Goodbye, Ah-Xing."

He could hear she was walking with a spring in her step. The footsteps echoed from an increasingly higher elevation as she climbed the stairs. Ah-Xing stood at the foot of the stairs, silently listening to the receding footsteps. Then the doorbell rang, and Chen jia meimei called out joyously: "Mom, I'm back!" The door opened and closed. Only then was Ah-Xing satisfied that he'd "see" her safely home. He turned and headed to his own home. On the way Ah-Xing could smell the lingering odor of mutton mixed with that of cumin. Touching the greasy spot on his cheek, he broke into a laugh that remained soundless in the night air.

VI   The Purple Rose

Yu Manli was back. When the work order was being written up at the counter, Xiao Lin made a point of putting her in Room 02, where the masseuse was a Ms. Yang. She was following the instructions of the manager, who did not want to see the reputation of the Heart Light Massage Center tarnished because of some unpleasantness between Ah-Xing and the customer. While "Heart Ligh" was not a well-known brand, it was always a good idea to keep one's name unsoiled.

After glancing at the work order, however, Yu Manli told Xiao Lin: "I want the masseur in Room 03, the one I had last time."

Xiao Lin said, with a startled look on her face: "Did you say you wanted Ah-Xing? You want him to work on you today?"

"I don't know what his name is. I just know he works in Room 03."

Xiao Lin crossed out Ms. Yang's work number on the work order and wrote in Ah-Xing's number. She was mystified when Yu Manli pressed her lips together, smothering a burgeoning grin, as she was handed the amended work order. Yu Manli thanked her with a smile and headed to the changing room.

This Yu Manli, who patronized Heart Light twice before, had left an indelible impression in Xiao Lin's mind because of her grotesque features. Yu Manli's hideous appearance was not helped by her mean temper, the icy tone in her voice, and the fact that she had never been seen to smile. She had a haughty, petulant manner as if everybody owed her money.

Or maybe she had built a protective shield around herself because she had never in her life felt loved, and had to fend off strangers' curious and mocking looks. Women with physical beauty often resort to a haughty, frosty veneer as a weapon to ward off unwanted advances and physical harm. This ugly woman also needed a defensive device, less against physical harm than for the protection of her vulnerable heart, for ugly women are arguably more vulnerable to emotional hurt than bodily harm. Maybe that was the explanation for Yu Manli's haughty, frosty and unsmiling demeanor.

Today, uncharacteristically, Yu Manli smiled and said "thanks." Her *Homo erectus pekinensis* face however showed no improvement with the smile. On the contrary the skin that stretched taut over the lower triangular region of her face became ridged with outwardly radiating wrinkles when her lips, which she normally pressed tightly together, opened by a crack with the smile, baring two rows of buckteeth. Probably her smiling face looked more hideous than when she cried. No wonder she never smiled. So there must be a compelling reason for her uncustomary smile today. What happy thought made her smile despite herself?

Five minutes later Yu Manli emerged from the changing room in her terrycloth robe and plastic slippers, making her way toward Room 03 from the far end of the corridor. Already apprised of what transpired by Ah-Mei, Ah-Xing could now hear footsteps in the corridor but they did not sound like Yu Manli's footsteps. She normally walked with a lassitude in her gait, lifting her feet as little as possible, so that her plastic slippers shuffled along the floor. She was apathetic, unable to summon enough energy to get angry or irritated. Ah-Xing was already an expert in recognizing Yu Manli's footsteps after her two previous visits. But the approaching footsteps sounded bouncy and lively. They were striking, not in speed or step width, but in how high the feet were lifted off the ground. There was a spring in her step; every step was measured and choreographed as if she was dancing.

When Ah-Xing attended the school for the blind, he took a music appreciation course in which the teacher played well-known songs from around the world. It was Ah-Xing's favorite class. For someone deprived of visual perception, music afforded a way to discover the color of blue sky and the seasonal changes that bring blossoming flowers and falling leaves.

When he got his first paycheck, he bought a stereo system and a set of CDs of famous songs. Listening to music became the mainstay of his entertainment. As a result Ah-Xing developed a good ear for music. The footsteps in the corridor, approaching with a certain grace, had the definite hallmark of a minuet.

He had several minuet classics on his CDs. This was definitely not a Beethoven, which conjured the image of a leisured, aimless amble through the rooms in one's own home. Nor was it a Bizet, which was a stroll through a field amid the chatter and chirrup of birds. It was a far cry from Mozart, which evoked the picture of aristocrats strutting about affectedly in a palatial setting.

What kind of minuet was it then? Yes, it was the G major minuet of Bach. It did not cause one to picture a home, a field or a palace, but rather a little hut inundated by sunlight. This hut was so small there was barely room to take even a few steps, but because it was bathed in sunshine, every step taken had a warmth and a spring to it. The person who was now walking toward his room was someone basking in the sun. He could detect an indolence belying a bright, buoyant mood. Only someone in a sunny mood would be able to dance a minuet in her plastic slippers.

Bach's minuet in G major came into the room. It was Yu Manli who initiated the greetings: "How are you!"

It was as if a ray of sunshine had flooded Ah-Xing's face, which instantly brightened.

Yu Manli wanted to continue the course of treatment for her back. She was in a much better mood than during the previous two visits and was markedly less reticent. Lying on her stomach with her face buried in the hollow in the massage bed, she asked in a muffled voice: "So your name is Ah-Xing?"

Ah-Xing said with a laugh: "My full name is Xu Shixing but people like to call me Ah-Xing."

"Then I will also call you Ah-Xing from now on."

Ah-Xing agreed readily. Without stopping his massaging, he remarked: "Before you came into this room, I almost thought it was someone else. Your footsteps were different. They sounded like dancing steps. It was really graceful."

There was no response from Yu Manli except a few satisfied moans. Ah-Xing, whose hands were kneading her neck at this moment, could feel the temperature of her skin suddenly warm up by a few degrees. That to Ah-Xing was a sign of blushing. But

Ah-Xing was sure she liked what he said of her; it was a compliment after all.

He thought he understood: such a surge of latent passion, of quietly suppressed excitement, manifested on the surface of the skin was most often observed in women with unexpressed happiness. It was like a flower that just burst into bloom, its moist, bedewed, creamy-smooth petals releasing a natural scent. But it was a measured, controlled release expressing self-pride, aloneness and subtlety. Ah-Xing rubbed and kneaded Yu Manli's back with gentleness. Under his hands the warm, moist body was like some kind of flower. Like...yes, like a rose, a rose ready to burgeon.

Ah-Xing remembered a visit to the center last Labor Day by local leaders who wanted to show they'd not forgotten working people like Ah-Xing, who didn't allow their physical disability to demoralize them. The visiting local dignitaries did a quick walk-through of the massage center, gave every masseur and masseuse a rose with a word of encouragement, and left.

Ah-Mei had to almost rub her nose in the petals before she was able to discover that the rose Ah-Xing received from the visiting local leaders was a purple one. She told Ah-Xing that her rose was pink and was prettier than his. Ah-Xing tried to imagine what the color purple was like. He carefully ran his hand over the rose wrapped in cellophane. There was a lone flower at the tip of a slender stem. He could tell by its shape that the flower had not fully opened. While there was no water on the surface of the petals, they felt laden with moisture. With its petals folded inward, the flower struck him as moody and pensive. But he was even more struck by its grace. So, purple was a color that was partly open and partly closed. It was a color that brought to mind both solitude and gracefulness. Purple was also a fragrance. Only, it was a subtle fragrance, so subtle that it vaporized the moment it came in contact with a crowd.

Now Ah-Xing associated purple with Yu Manli. To him she was a purple rose that had not fully opened. He blurted out: "Manli, your skin is like the petal of a rose, a purple rose."

Yu Manli's skin did indeed feel like a petal and smell like a flower. She seemed skeptical though: "A purple rose? Have you ever seen one?"

It was of course a gaffe on her part. How could she put such a question to a blind person? She sounded as if she was mocking his inability to see. But Ah-Xing was not annoyed or upset. With his head slightly upturned and to one side, and two expressionless eyes, he maintained a serene, unperturbed look on his rectangular face. She thought: "If not for his blindness, this man would be considered handsome. But if he was a seeing person, would he still tell me I have a beautiful face?" Thankfully he was blind.

Perhaps somewhat saddened by the thought, Yu Manli fell silent. To Yu Manli, any healthy pair of eyes was a weapon of cruel, devastating power. It was however unrealistic to wish everybody was afflicted with blindness. Maybe the only remedy was to go blind herself so that she would not be able to see how ugly she was. But an ugly woman has the same fond hopes as a pretty woman: to be pampered, complimented and fall in love, or even to make an occasional visit for a facial massage, which would be a form of self-approbation. Oh would that she had at least a plain face if stunning beauty was not meant for her!

Yu Manli must have her dreams too, modest dreams; maybe all she hoped for was to be able to walk into places such as a beauty parlor without feeling self-conscious. Centers like this with blind masseurs were a godsend. They were perfect for her because the service providers were blind and therefore could not see the appearance of their clients. Exactly what she needed!

But a majority of these establishments claimed to be staffed by the blind only to obtain the preferential tax treatment reserved for not-for-profit service organizations. They either had no blind staff at or had no blind masseurs. It was only when she stumbled on the Heart Light Massage Center that she had her first encounter with a real blind masseur. And on her second visit, when she had a head massage, the masseur in Room 03 had said to her:

"Manli, you have a very beautiful face!"

Tears had started streaming down her face.

If this compliment had come from a seeing person, Yu Manli would most probably have thought he was mocking her. But Ah-Xing could not see her; he must judge beauty very differently. Ah-Xing's judgment relied on his senses of hearing and touch. Clearly his criteria were not recognized by most people, but they were one kind of criteria nonetheless. Suppose all the people of the world were blind. Then by these criteria wouldn't Yu Manli be recognized as a beauty?

Yu Manli had a good cry lying in the massage bed. One imagines she must have been crying because when an ugly woman like her was complimented on her beauty it finally released that feminine desire, buried deep in her heart, to look pretty. And there might be other, obscure reasons for the torrent of tears. Ah-Xing did not ask her why she was crying, confident that he had not hurt her feelings with some careless remarks. Nor were her tears those of hurt. She was crying because her emotions got the better of her. An enormous joy swelled her heart to the point of opening the floodgates of tears. They were tears of joy.

Ah-Xing uttered not a word but kept wiping off the tears that streamed down her face until she finally stopped sobbing and made a sheepish apology. Only then did he say with a smile: "Not to worry. Tears are good for your complexion."

Yu Manli couldn't suppress a laugh at these words. Then she asked: "On my next visit can I ask for you by name?"

"Of course you can. No problem."

That day when Yu Manli left, her eyes were red and swollen, but her mood couldn't have been sunnier.

VII   The Longing of the Skin

By now Ah-Xing had accumulated substantial experience in perceiving women. The earliest impression, naturally, was of his mother before he reached the age of eight. He vaguely recalled his mother's limp, wispy hair, her cold and rigid hands and feet, and the shortness of breath invariably present in her voice, even when she talked in her sleep. It was later confirmed they all were symptoms of anemia.

Ah-Xing had no deep attachment to his mother, a frail woman both physically and emotionally, so frail that she showed apathy toward everything around her. Debilitated by her illness, she had difficulty even taking care of herself. She died very young.

Using the analogy of colors, he would describe his mother as a colorless woman. Maybe Ah-Xing at that young age had not yet developed the brain cells necessary for his method of translating color perception. In contrast, the women in his life now had definite colors. His sister-in-law, who emanated a gentleness and warmth and had small, fleshy hands, was associated in his mind with the color of ash gray. Then there was the affectionate, outgoing Ah-Mei, who liked to wear pretty dresses. She was the color of bright red. The irrepressible, loud-mouthed Chen jia meimei was the color orange, but could easily turn another color without warning. And Yu Manli, the lonely, poised, somewhat aloof Yu Manli, the color purple.

He always paired colors with women, with one color assigned to every woman he knew. Or put another way, every woman he knew could be compared to some color. Colors did not exist in Ah-Xing's brain as visual impressions, only abstract concepts. Whenever he heard any word associated with a color, Ah-Xing had to find something that he could touch or hear to serve as the representative of that color. And in women, Ah-Xing had finally found the ideal surrogates for colors.

Women still remained an abstract concept to Ah-Xing, who could not grasp why women were women although he had heard them talk and worked on their skin, muscles and bones. Just as he had no idea what colors were, despite the fact that he knew the associations between red and pain, orange-yellow and heat, ash gray and warmth, purple and coolness.

That's why Ah-Xing drew parallels between women and colors—two abstract concepts whose essence would forever be beyond his ken.

As far as Ah-Xing was concerned, the moment a woman walked into the Heart Light Massage Center, she was no longer a woman but strictly a customer. Ah-Xing treated a woman with the attention of a professional masseur, as he would treat any of his customers. He was attentive to the subtlest tactile sensation, the faintest sound emitted, because they could be factors in understanding and analyzing the customer. If he were a masseur with healthy eyes, he would probably derive more information from visual observations, and there's no denying that even the most pure-hearted men tend to look at women in a particular way.

Ah-Xing was normal as a man. He therefore was extra attentive when dealing with female clients, who tended to drop their guard because of his blindness. Most of the female clients came for Ah-Xing's professional skills. They felt safe with him and yet deep down they were contemptuous of him. Ah-

Xing already tried his best to behave like a person with no physical handicaps. They thought him a gentleman, and a handsome one at that, but he was a blind person after all.

So while these women enjoyed the massage given by his expert hands, he inspired in them a sense of pity and sympathy, which boiled down to contempt—a blind person! For this reason his female clients, once sprawled on the massage bed, became, without exception, mutes. They felt no need to engage him in conversation; the only sounds they emitted were the satisfied moans from their pampered bodies. To all intents and purposes he simply didn't exist. What woman would allow a healthy man to hear the sounds she makes when she yawns and stretches or sneezes, or even those heard only when she relieves herself? The ladies didn't care whether they looked good or not in front of this Ah-Xing. They wanted to exhibit their beauty only to men with normal sight. Yu Manli was the only exception. Well, there was also now Chen jia meimei, except that she was a woman unrelated to

Heart Light. No, not a woman—Chen jia meimei could only be considered a child.

That night when Chen jia meimei planted a kiss on Ah-Xing's cheek, piously performing an act of what she described as "kissing goodbye," he had entertained the idea of not seeing her anymore. But now thanks to that kiss, smelling powerfully of mutton and cumin, he put that thought to rest. It was as if the kiss triggered a longing in Ah-Xing's skin.

Many were the people whose skin had been massaged by Ah-Xing but his skin had never been touched by anybody. That was not completely true; his mother must have caressed him when he was little, but that memory had long faded. His sister-in-law had rubbed his head and put her arm around his shoulder from time to time, but that stopped when he grew up. Except for that once when he came in contact with his sister-in-law's hand when he accepted the sweater from her. But that was an unintended, momentary contact.

If Ah-Xing perceived emotion through his skin,

then certainly he gave more affection, in the form of touching, than he received in his adult life. The ears perceive things at a distance; the skin, in contrast, provides intimate, direct contact. How could his skin not experience affection? Ah-Xing's skin had feelings even for things such as the air, sunshine, rain, fog and dew. When Chen jia meimei kissed him goodbye, she awakened the affection that had lain latent, imprisoned all these years in Ah-Xing's skin.

Granny Yan came to him to deliver a message: "Ah-Xing, Chen jia meimei is very happy with you. Her mother says Ah-Xing is very smart despite his blindness. She says her daughter has good eyes, so you complement each other."

Ah-Xing smiled but did not say anything. Granny Yan went on: "After you get married, you can have a baby that combines your smarts and her good eyes. Wouldn't that be great! I would have fulfilled my duty then."

Ah-Xing thought: "We don't need another child. Chen jia meimei is one already."

Granny Yan continued: "Ah-Xing, if you have

no objection to this match, why don't you pay a visit to the Chen family next week?"

"Why should I pay them a visit?"

Granny Yan said with a laugh: "Why pay them a visit? You'll become the son-in-law to be—the Chen family's *maojiao nuxu*—after the visit."

Ah-Xing's ears were now inundated by Granny Yan's stream of well-meaning exhortations: what presents the future son-in-law should bring, what he should wear, what should and should not be said. His mind was somewhere else however. He was replaying that energetic kiss planted on his cheek by Chen jia meimei.

How could he characterize that feeling? It was so sudden, out of the blue, a little tingling, sweet. Definitely an unusual experience. Wouldn't it be a display of frivolity if he was to agree to marriage simply because of that one kiss? Ah-Xing felt torn. He clearly liked, even yearned for, that kind of feeling. On the other hand he might not have any real feeling of love for Chen jia meimei. But that tantalizing kiss had stirred a thirst for something more.

Faced with Ah-Xing's reluctance to give a definitive answer, Granny Yan asked: "Ah-Xing, tell me the truth. Do you or do you not like Chen jia meimei?"

Ah-Xing couldn't answer that question. If he answered yes, he would feel he was making a lousy bargain. To say no would mean he had to give her up, which he was not ready to do. He was reduced to mumbling. Granny Yan said: "I'll go see your elder brother and his wife and ask them to talk some sense into you."

The day of that first visit as the son-in-law to be came soon. Ah-Xing's sister-in-law took it upon herself to prepare all the presents: a basket of top-quality fruits; two bottles of *Nao Bai Jin*, an expensive melatonin supplement; a Nestle coffee gift set; and a bouquet of flowers. Delivering them to Ah-Xing's place early in the morning, she cautioned him: "If out of politeness the Chen family asks you to stay for supper, don't commit the social blunder of accepting the invitation. At the first visit, the important thing is to get a feel for the girl's upbringing. If there's anything that bothers you after the visit, be sure to tell me. Do you understand?"

"I understand." But he thought to himself: "I don't want to go. My elder brother and my sister-in-law are making me go."

That was a bit disingenuous. He was trying to deny, or he was reluctant to admit, that he liked Chen jia meimei. Or to be more precise, he actually disliked the girl who'd never grow up, who couldn't open her mouth without rhapsodizing about Andy Lau. What he liked was a tactile sensation: the unfamiliar, intriguing feeling of feminine skin next to his own.

VIII   The Touch of a Hand

The fruits and fresh-cut flowers piled on the dining table filled Ah-Xing's nostrils with a mixture of aromas. He felt every present one by one, and when his hand touched the cellophane wrapping of the flowers, he brought his nose closer and inhaled deeply. By the smell he could tell there were roses in the bunch. He was not disappointed. After gingerly feeling every single flower he pulled out a rose on its stem, ready to bloom, and put it carefully in an inside pocket of his jacket before buttoning up.

With the rose tucked close to this chest, Ah-Xing made his way toward Heart Light. It was a Wednesday. Yu Manli had made an appointment for a back massage that day. She already completed four of the eight sessions of treatment. This would be her fifth. Normally Yu Manli would arrive about ten in the morning and was never late. Ah-Xing would wait for her on such days, declining other work orders, telling the customers to either come back another day or get their treatment from Master Mao in Room 01 or Ms. Yang in Room 02.

Every masseur had loyal customers. Ah-Xing had a large following, including people such as Mr. Wang, the seafood wholesaler, Mr. Li, a real estate agent, and Ms. Liu, who owned a game room. Yu Manli was a relative newcomer to his fan club, but in barely a month she had rapidly risen to the top of

Ah-Xing's list of favorite customers.

Ah-Xing enjoyed massaging Yu Manli because this woman had a face like no other, a face that his hands judged as beautiful. Another reason was her skin, which had the fine and smooth texture and subtle fragrance of the petals of a purple rose. But the most important reason was that he could detect a change in Yu Manli, who had undergone a metamorphosis from the aloofness of the first visit, to the sobbing of the second, to a mood that became cheerier through the third and fourth sessions. In the process she mellowed a lot and became more willing to engage him in conversation. Ah-Xing was reasonably sure that the changes in Yu Manli had to do with his performance as a professional masseur. Even if it proved otherwise, he was still gratified by these changes in her. What counted for him was that Yu Manli was the only customer who had confided in him. The first time he found her face streaming with tears, Ah-Xing felt an inexplicable sympathy welling up in him. From that moment on, this customer dubbed "Peking Man" by Xiao Lin and Ah-Mei had been receiving special treatment from Ah-Xing.

Punctually at quarter past ten, Yu Manli arrived. There was no mistaking the minuet footsteps. Ah-Xing smiled in his heart and his facial muscles relaxed. Ah-Mei recognized the sound too: "Peking Man is here!"

Ah-Xing chided her: "Don't give the customers nicknames."

Ah-Mei said with a giggle: "I won't call her that to her face."

"You can't call her that behind her back either. If it became known, people would think poorly of the employees of this center."

Ah-Mei was resentful: "Why are you so nice to her? She's not even your girlfriend."

Before he could deliver a rebuttal, Yu Manli had opened the door and walked into the room. After an exchange of greetings, she lay down as was the routine, and Ah-Xing settled in the chair at the head of the bed to begin the therapy, starting with her back.

Yu Manli appeared to be in a cheery mood. Her

voice streamed from the hollow in which her face was buried to reach Ah-Xing's ears: "Ah-Xing, what is your favorite type of music?"

Ah-Xing rolled his eyes, showing the whites, his head at a slight angle. "I, I think I like all kinds of music."

"Do you like 'Moon Reflected in the Erquan Spring'?"

"Yes, '*Erquan Yingyue*' is one of my favorites. It was composed by Ah-Bing, a blind person like me."

As he said this, he could feel Yu Manli raising her head. He stopped his massage, thinking Yu Manli was going to adjust her posture. Instead, she sat up in the massage bed and pressed a small, thin plastic case into his hand. Ah-Xing could tell it was a CD. Yu Manli resumed her prone posture. "This is a gift for you. It's a CD of traditional Chinese folk music."

Holding the CD between his fingers, Ah-Xing said: "Thank you, Manli. But we are not allowed to accept gifts from our customers."

In a clear voice, Yu Manli said: "Then don't

think of me as a customer, but as a friend. You can accept a gift from a friend, can't you?"

"It's okay from a friend."

Then he remembered the rose in the inside pocket of his jacket. He unbuttoned his white coat to take out the flower, which was warm from having been kept close to his skin. "I have a gift for you too, Manli."

Raising her head, Yu Manli saw a torn purple rose thrust at her face.

"Here, this is for you."

The rose had languished in his pocket for quite some time. It was further damaged as it was extracted from the pocket, and it drooped, with several petals missing and the rest hanging limply. Yu Manli laughed and took the rose with one hand, unable to stop her merriment. Ah-Xing laughed with her, not knowing why she was laughing. But you can't go wrong laughing, so he dutifully joined in.

Yu Manli finally stopped laughing. "Why did you give me a rose?"

"Because to my mind you are like a rose."

Ah-Xing was simply and innocently describing his feelings. He had no idea what subtle effects his words would have on his listener. Yu Manli's face was now all flushed. Changes in emotions prompted by inner thoughts have a way of expressing themselves outwardly on the human skin. He could sense the sudden rise in temperature on Yu Manli's neck. That must mean she was blushing. Kneading her burning nape, Ah-Xing felt his palm heating up too.

After a silent interval, Yu Manli said: "Did you buy this rose?"

Ah-Xing could not tell a lie. "I didn't. My sister-in-law bought it."

"Your sister-in-law? Why would she buy roses for you?" Yu Manli's curiosity was piqued.

Using the fragments of information gleaned from Ah-Xing's muttered, evasive answer together with a healthy dose of her imagination, Yu Manli was able to put together the story behind the rose.

Instead of pursuing the subject, she dropped her face back into the hollow and abandoned her back to the attentive hands of Ah-Xing. More than halfway into the session, Ah-Mei's light, brisk footsteps sounded in the corridor, and she popped into the room in time to hear Ah-Xing say to Yu Manli: "How should I thank you for the music CD you gave me? Why don't I offer you a bonus service, say a head massage or an ear candle? Pick one."

Tugging the front of her terrycloth robe tighter, Yu Manli turned over and lay face up. "All right, give me a head massage then. Thank you, Ah-Xing."

Ah-Mei interjected: "Ah-Xing, Mr. Niu, the owner of that construction business, is here. He says he has an appointment with you."

Without turning his head, Ah-Xing said: "Ask Mr. Niu to be kind enough to get either Master Mao or Ms. Yang to do him today, whoever is available."

Ah-Mei did not like the idea one bit and her unfocused eyes briefly flickered. She turned around and stalked out of the room, slamming the door and leaving behind a sudden hush, breached only by the breathing of Ah-Xing and Yu Manli. They did not utter a word, one lying face up with eyes closed and the other busily pulling from the work cart his bottles of protein cream, almond ointment, menthol oil and facial masks. There was a pause following the clinking sounds as if he were taking a deep breath. Then he stretched out his hands and started working with precision and deftness on her face.

The moment his hands touched skin in a professional manner, all feelings of confusion and disquiet left him. Besides, there was nothing ordinary or boring about Yu Manli's head and face. With most men and women, the differences were normally matters of degree between rough and fine, big and small. Yu Manli's face however was not your run-of-the-mill face. When Ah-Xing had done a head massage for her before, he realized for the first time that there were mountains and valleys and winding roads on a human face just as in a landscape. It was hard to characterize this richness of features. It was after all his first encounter with such a unique face, and he was just like a mathematician mulling over a challenging theorem or a climber preparing for an ascent of Everest. The proving of the theorem and the scaling of Everest presented challenges, but it was the challenge that filled him with curiosity and a will to conquer.

Ah-Xing's hands moved with the utmost gentleness and deliberation from the chin longitudinally to the forehead, from the center of the brow across the face to the earlobes, describing an arc from the side of the nose to the cheekbone and from the crown of the head toward the circumference of the cranium. Always going with the grain of the muscles and bones, he continued until every inch of the head and the face was covered.

Yu Manli's face was thus repeatedly and meticulously traced by his hands. It occurred to Ah-Xing that if all those ordinary faces he'd ever touched were solo performances, then Yu Manli's face would best be described as a symphony rich in tonality and instrumental sophistication. He would even go so far as to ascribe a story line to that symphony of a face, with every distinct feature representing a mini-crescendo in the music. It was a pastoral poem tinged with melancholy, exhibiting the beauty not of a plain but of a landscape ringed with soaring, sheer, jagged mountain peaks. This was a musical work that was iconoclastic and creative, accessible to a select few and often dismissed as mere noise at first hearing. But a listener with an attentive ear would find beauty precisely in the conflicts and clashes.

Ah-Xing knew that he was one of the select few who could appreciate this symphony. In fact he was at this very moment appreciating her, his hands acquiring the rhythm of the music, feeling the pulsing of every note. Over and over he replicated the aesthetic experience with his loving hands. Rhapsodic, he cried out: "So beautiful!"

Lying face up in the massage bed, Yu Manli asked: "What's beautiful?"

Startled out of his reverie, Ah-Xing answered: "Manli, your face. It's like a symphony. It's so beautiful."

Yu Manli laughed self-disparagingly: "Ah-Xing, you wouldn't say that if you could see me."

Ah-Xing laughed with her: "Who says I can't see? The two eyes in my face may be out of commission but I have a third eye in my mind, and it can see the beauty of your face."

As he said this, Ah-Xing thought that what people see with their eyes is often just the surface, just appearances. They rely too heavily on their eyes. The truth is you penetrate more easily to the essence of beauty when you have no eyes to rely on. So he said to Yu Manli: "People are easily deceived by their eyes."

He almost sounded like a philosopher to be able to make such a pithy statement. But his comment elicited a long sigh from Yu Manli. Ah-Xing, who had been working on Yu Manli's earlobes, moved on to the sides of her neck. Her joints and connective tissues, like rusted cogwheels newly lubricated, made faint, crisp sounds as they started turning again. But that feminine sigh was not one of pleasure from the loosening of rigid joints, muscles and ligaments. It was a sigh commingled with a trace of wistfulness. Before he could ask if she was feeling unwell, Yu Manli stretched out a hand and gently grabbed the hand that was rubbing her neck just below the chin.

Yu Manli's warm and moist hand held Ah-

Xing's hand for a good long while. At first Ah-Xing,
startled, allowed Yu Manli to hold on to his hand.
Recovering from the initial shock moments later, he
tried to free his hand from her grip. But the attempt
did not translate into real action. Ah-Xing could
clearly sense a mild tremor in the woman's soft hand,
and an electric current, as it were, flowing from her
body to his in pulsating waves. Soon that warm,
moist, suppressed excitement infected Ah-Xing's
hand, triggering a tingling sensation as all his pores
opened up, as if thirsting for the nutrients passed
from the woman's skin to his.

Ah-Xing did not extricate his hand from
Yu Manli's grip. Instead, his hand was becoming
ambivalent. It was hard to resist the temptation of
intimate contact with a feminine hand. So Ah-Xing's
hand stayed captive in Yu Manli's for three seconds,
five seconds, eight seconds...and then Ah-Xing felt
a current of air rising slowly from within his core,
heading straight up and gradually spreading to blot
out this unreal, otherworldly feeling. When the
rising current hit his cheeks, there was a momentary

tingling, and two puddles of stinging tears appeared in Ah-Xing's vacant eyes.

IX   Awakening

The treatment session lasted for a full two and a half hours that day. By the time it ended Ah-Xing had already missed lunch hour and the lunch box ordered by the massage center for him had gone cold. Ah-Mei said: "Ah-Xing, do you want me to reheat your lunch in the microwave?"

"Don't bother. I'm taking the afternoon off to take care of a few things at home."

As he left the center, Ah-Xing bid goodbye to Xiao Lin, who was trimming her nails at the checkout counter. She caught a glimpse of his red, swollen eyes. Naturally Ah-Xing had no way of knowing the difference a few tears in his blind eyes would make in his appearance. He was not in the mood to continue working that day. He just wanted to go home, to be by himself and think about things without being distracted.

This was early afternoon and there was a lull in the streets as he headed home. Most of the residences along the way had their doors closed, but not necessarily because the retired folks were taking a siesta. From the few households whose doors remained open came the distinct sounds of mahjongg tiles being shuffled, and frail-voiced but sharp arguments about minor infractions of the rules or petty sums of money won or lost. The retirees from the households with closed doors were out in other homes forming foursomes to play mahjongg. The elderly of this city were fond of this game in which only small sums of money changed hands, and they went about it openly and unapologetically. They apparently felt that their contribution to the city during their life entitled them to the enjoyment of the time and space afforded them in their retirement. This game, which was either unavailable or unaffordable to them in their younger years, was making a roaring comeback. Suddenly realizing all the good times they'd missed, they were now, in their golden years, indulging in the game with a vengeance to make up for lost time.

In these hours of the afternoon lull, the usual roving peddlers who worked the streets and back alleys silenced their hawking. The drivers, often disabled people, of three-wheeled cabs had gone home to nap, the raucous honking of their horns now silenced. The quiet was punctured by a powerful motorcycle zooming by. This motorbike rider must be some young man out to have fun or to meet a date who was anxiously awaiting him somewhere. Against the backdrop of the early afternoon calm, the roaring of this lone bike sounded particularly forlorn, like the tragic intoning of a lyric tenor in an opera—an exposé of a brief but brilliant life, followed by a burst of obnoxious fumes from the tailpipe, before the exit backstage.

Ah-Xing was again on the sidewalk path reserved for the blind. He had come to know by heart this path leading to his home. There was the herringbone tile where the square tiles gave way to the round ones. This tile with a one-of-a-kind pattern had become like a way station for him. On his way to and from work, Ah-Xing normally kept an even pace but when he came to this herringbone tile, a brief hesitation was noticeable in his gait. It was an imperceptible half-beat pause in an arpeggio played by a pianist, the time it took a drop of water to fall into a cup. In this twinkling of an eye a whimsical thought would sometimes creep into his mind. However these reveries invariably dissipated the moment he resumed his normal pace.

But on this day Ah-Xing came to a complete halt as he reached the herringbone tile. He planted both feet on the tile and turned to face the street, allowing the afternoon sunshine to flood his shoulders. He asked himself if he still wanted to visit the Chen household this evening. He hadn't before had the luxury of looking at such matters from all possible angles, taking account of all conceivable factors. For him it was always a case of accepting whatever came his way when the time was right—the melon that had ripened on the vine and fallen into his lap—as long as he felt no particular revulsion toward what he was getting. At all critical junctures in his life, everything arranged itself and fell into place: getting an education, graduating, getting a job. He was never called on to make a decision. His lack of experience would not qualify him to make one the first place.

He counted himself as lucky to have been born in this city, where relative affluence meant that people in good health had the spare time to care about disabled people like him. In time he became a poster boy for the do-gooders because he had the advantage of being better endowed than most other disabled people. As a matter of fact, the death of his parents in his early childhood aside, he never lacked care and attention. He had received a kind of general, but sincere, affection, although not of the extraordinary, passionate nature. Therefore he was devoid of any profound, intense craving for love.

But it was different now. This was a very special day in his life, and he had to stop to think with a clear head. If life was like a road, then the encountering a woman was surely a stop on that road.

If the kiss planted on his cheek by Chen jia

meimei triggered in Ah-Xing a craving for the intimacy of the skin, then Yu Manli's holding of his hand had churned up from the depths of his heart the long suppressed craving for love he never even knew was there.

Chen jia meimei's kiss on his cheek awakened in him a feeling of joy, happiness and a desire for more. Admittedly a kiss is usually more of an expression of love than holding hands. But when Yu Manli held his hand in hers, he was thrown into a fluster. His heart palpitated and he did not have the strength to break free. When it was over, a wave of melancholy washed over him. This was no longer an affliction of the skin but one that attacked vital organs.

After long consideration Ah-Xing decided that it would be out of the question for him to visit the Chen household as a future son-in-law, pretending that nothing had happened. It suddenly occurred to him that he had never thought of joining the Chen household as act of love but merely a matter of acquiring new relations. Nor had he thought that plucking one rose from the bouquet intended for the Chen family and giving it to Yu Manli would have any consequences. Just as the local leaders distributed roses to workers like him on national holidays, he was also using the rose as a means of communication, of showing appreciation for someone. He was pleased by the changes produced as a result of his professional work in Yu Manli as she cheered up more and more with each session. She gave him a sense of fulfillment and for that he wanted to show his gratitude. The rose was a token of that gratitude and a reaffirmation of the color assigned to her in his imagination. Didn't he liken Yu Manli to a purple rose?

Tonight, however, Yu Manli had shed her shell of customer and triggered an awakening in Ah-Xing in her new guise as a woman. Or did his rose awaken her first and she in turn caused his awakening? Regardless of who awakened whom, the fact was that Ah-Xing was roused from his innocence. He might not have become fully awake but he was no longer in a baseline state. He stood for a long time on that tile in the blind path lost in thought. His brain was now like a pot of soup, rich in nutrients that his body was barely able to digest and absorb.

Ah-Xing remained standing for over an hour on the sidewalk until the regular noises of the city returned—peddlers hawking their wares, honking of horns, small groups of retired workers chatting. He finally resumed his walk home.

At four in the afternoon, Granny Yan telephoned him: "Ah-Xing, do you have a pair of sunglasses? If not, I'll bring a pair so that you can wear them when we call on the Chen family."

Ah-Xing said with hesitation: "Granny Yan, I don't think I should go."

Granny Yan said scoldingly: "Nonsense! Why the sudden change of mind? Everything has been arranged."

Ah-Xing racked his brain to find an excuse for not going: "I'm sure Chen jia muma and Chen jia baba will be put off by my blindness."

Granny Yan laughed: "Ah-Xing, it's not as if Chen jia muma never met you. She was pleased with you; that's why they want you to visit. Have confidence in yourself!"

Ah-Xing hastened to add: "Chen jia meimei is for all practical purposes just a child. I don't think she's suitable for me."

Granny Yan took umbrage: "Ah-Xing, you can't go back on your word. You promised them! And now you want to back out of it. You are making me, the matchmaker, look bad. You must go tonight. After tonight, I'll wash my hands of it. Stay put and I'll come and get you right away."

Before Ah-Xing could protest, Granny Yan had already hung up. Twenty minutes later, she arrived in a hurried manner and proceeded to make Ah-Xing change his clothes and comb his hair. She then produced a pair of sun glasses for Ah-Xing to wear. Taking two steps backward, she surveyed the result, looking Ah-Xing up and down before saying with relief: "Ah-Xing, you look really handsome with the sunglasses! Quit troubling yourself with silly thoughts. I hate to say this, but it's hard to find a match for someone with your handicap."

Ah-Xing nodded, for he had to admit he fully agreed with Granny Yan's observation.

X   The Visit

Ah-Xing followed Granny Yan out the door, carrying the four gifts. The Chen family lived only a short distance away. They went up the stairs and rang the doorbell. The sound of footsteps in the apartment was followed by Chen jia muma's enthusiastic greetings: "Hello, Granny Yan! Hello, Ah-Xing! Come right in!"

This was immediately followed by the ringing, childlike voice of Chen jia meimei, who had appeared out of nowhere: "Ah-Xing, Ah-Xing, you look so handsome in those sunglasses!"

Chen jia muma and Granny Yan exchanged a furtive, knowing smile. A man with a rattle in his throat spoke up in a hoarse voice: "Granny Yan! Thank you for all you've done. Please have a seat!"

Granny Yan said to Ah-Xing: "This is Chen jia

baba, the father of the family."

Ah-Xing turned in the direction of the hoarse, male voice and spoke reverentially: "Chen jia baba, how do you do?"

Chen jia meimei couldn't wait to drag Ah-Xing toward the interior of the apartment, saying: "Ah-Xing, come to my room. I'll show you pictures of Andy Lau."

It was as if Ah-Xing's feet had struck roots into the floor, for he stayed anchored, not budging an inch no matter how hard Chen jia meimei pulled. Her mother said: "Ah-Xing, go! It's all right. From now on our place is your place, so make yourself at home."

Encouraged by her mother's support, Chen jia meimei dragged harder and finally got Ah-Xing to move. Chen jia muma reminded her daughter: "Meimei, Ah-Xing can't see the pictures, so you'll explain them to him, okay?"

She answered briskly: "Okay!"

Once in her room Chen jia meimei sat Ah-Xing down in a chair and got out a pile of pictures from a drawer: "Ah-Xing, I'm going to explain them to you now. Listen carefully."

As promised, she explained with great patience one picture after another: Andy Lau at a concert on such and such a date; Andy Lau in one of his movie roles; Andy Lau at a fund-raising charity concert... Ah-Xing listened half-heartedly but the initial awkwardness had eased significantly. After finishing her narration of the pictures, Chen jia meimei thrust a baby doll into his lap, saying: "Ah-Xing, this is my favorite doll. I'll let you hold it."

Feeling with his hands, Ah-Xing determined it was a bare-bottomed plastic doll with a big head, flat nose, small eyes and puffy cheeks. Unlike most other dolls, it was almost grotesque. Intrigued, Ah-Xing explored the ugly baby with his hands. This pleased Chen jia meimei, who asked: "Ah-Xing, do you find the ugly baby interesting?"

Ah-Xing nodded: "Yes, it is interesting."

"Last time my dad took me to the Yaohan Department Store to buy me toys, I wanted to get this ugly baby. Dad said it looked so hideous it might scare people to death. He said I should pick a pretty one, but I insisted on this one because I liked how it looked. Ah-Xing, do you like the ugly baby?"

Ah-Xing nodded again: "I like it."

"Then I'll give the ugly baby to you."

Ah-Xing shook his head vehemently. "No, no! This is your doll. It's your favorite. Keep it for yourself."

Chen jia meimei suddenly remembered the agreement she made with him. "Ah-Xing, I have not told people Xu Shixing is my boyfriend. I've kept my word, haven't I?"

A corner of Ah-Xing's mouth twitched in an involuntary smile. Chen jia meimei continued: "Ah-Xing, you also kept your word because you didn't tell my mom that you bought me ice cream, popcorn and shish kebabs. So we both kept our word, right?"

Ah-Xing humored her: "Yes, we both did."

Chen jia meimei thought of something else: "My mom said I should follow Ah-Xing's example and be able to support myself. She also said that Ah-Xing is very smart, even smarter than people who can see."

That made him blush. Deep down he felt a surge of pride and satisfaction, although he shook his head and said self-deprecatingly: "I am not smart. You are smarter than I am, and you'll be able to support yourself. That's for certain."

While what Ah-Xing said did not reflect reality, he was not lying. He actually meant it. Talking with her was like talking to a child, and this sudden regression to a form of dialogue used only when speaking with children was relaxing and fun for him. In the eyes of Chen jia meimei, Ah-Xing was the second most admired person, next to Andy Lau. The admiration might well have been the consequence of her mother constantly drumming it into her head, as well as Ah-Xing's treating her to ice cream and other snacks. But even so, the admiration warmed Ah-Xing's heart. Chen jia meimei and her mother were both so kind to him. He had to admit that this was a nice family.

After more than an hour spent in Chen jia meimei's room, he heard Chen jia muma's offer to have them stay for supper. Granny Yan said: "Maybe next time, but not today." That was the cue for Ah-Xing to go home. As he got up to leave, Chen jia meimei quickly whispered into his ear: "Ah-Xing, take me to the Jinjiang Theme Park one of these days. Oh, and I am still hungry for those mutton shish kebabs, but don't tell mom."

Just as she finished that sentence, Chen jia meimei put her arms around Ah-Xing's neck and gave his left cheek a loud smack. And before Ah-Xing had time to react, she planted another big one on his right cheek. Then she cackled with laughter. Ah-Xing, left speechless, walked out of the room in a daze.

The visitors had just departed and were out in the stairwell, when the apartment door was thrown open again. Chen jia meimei rushed out to press the ugly doll into Ah-Xing's hand before running back home. At the door she turned and called out in a loud voice: "Ah-Xing, see you next time."

Chen jia muma and Granny Yan both laughed. Clutching the ugly baby doll, Ah-Xing turned his head toward the voice of Chen jia meimei and answered softly and with a brief smile: "See you."

Once they were outside the apartment building, Granny Yan said: "Ah-Xing, don't dilly dally anymore. The Chen family is serious about you. Where else are you going to find another family that will accept you as they've done? It's settled then."

Ah-Xing's mouth twitched but only indistinct, unintelligible sounds came out of it.

It was another sleepless night. Lying in his bed, he tried to remember the feeling he had when Yu Manli took his hand into hers that morning in the massage room. What happened only a few hours ago now suddenly seemed to have taken place in faraway childhood. He even began to suspect that the ten seconds of hand holding with Yu Manli had been all in his imagination, a mere illusion.

In order to convince himself, he repeatedly went over in his mind what happened during the entire massage session that morning, reviewing meticulously every minute of the two and half hours. He reconstructed bit by bit that feeling of agitation and of being torn between resistance and temptation. With the memory coming back to him, his heart, too, relived the tingling, pulsating, nerve-racking excitement. Yes, that was the feeling he had had; it all became clearer now. It couldn't have been his imagination, for that very afternoon he had thought about canceling the visit to the Chen family and breaking up with Chen jia meimei.

Now that he had rediscovered that feeling, he was convinced it was no illusion.

What kind of feeling was it then? Ah-Xing would not dare utter the word "love," not even in the privacy of his own head. He only suspected, or guessed, that an unusual kind of affection had quietly taken possession of him. How else to explain this reluctance to forget?

While only that afternoon he had bathed in the thrill of Yu Manli's making, in the evening he had found himself enveloped in the warmth of the hearth and home of the Chen family. Ah-Xing found that he truly liked the homey atmosphere there. Even if Chen jia meimei stayed a child and never learned to appreciate true romantic love, Ah-Xing would not count it against her or feel ashamed of her. He liked being relied on and needed by her, and being looked up to as a model of intelligence and self-reliance. It scarcely mattered if her needing him was based on ice cream, shish kebabs and Andy Lau. Chen jia meimei made him feel like an able man and forget his own blindness. With her, he never felt any low self-esteem.

"What do you want then?" Ah-Xing kept asking himself. There was total confusion in his mind. After a while, he decided that his emotional attachment to Yu Manli was unrealistic. She was only a customer. Even if she had cried in front of him and had held his hand for a while, he still didn't know anything about her true identity, her past, profession or marital status. Who was she? He knew nothing about her.

Yu Manli, Yu Manli, this purple rose of a woman. Ah-Xing sighed resignedly. Finally, with the first chirping of the birds he grew groggy and fell asleep. Outwardly peaceful, his sleep proved fitful. As the day's noises grew louder, he drifted in and out of consciousness.

XI   The Promise of a Pleasant Surprise

These days Ah-Xing's heart was clearly not in his work at the massage center. Between ten in the morning and noontime, he refused to take any customers. No one except Ah-Xing himself knew the reason. He was in a constant state of suspense, expecting Yu Manli to walk into the Heart Light Massage Center some morning when least expected.

In Ah-Xing's imagination, he pictured how Yu Manli would glide into Room 03 to the beat of a minuet. What would she do or say after she came in? What gestures would she make other than taking his hand in hers? Even thinking about it produced a stirring in his heart followed by a vague worry. His mood vacillated between sweetness and agony, but mostly sweetness. Ah-Xing thought, this must be what people call a love triangle, or, as the Chinese called it, "straddling two boats." When he thought of that, the worry overwhelmed the sweetness.

Thus Ah-Xing waited, immersed in his reveries, and another Wednesday was soon upon him.

But on this Wednesday Yu Manli did not show up in her customary time slot. There was still no sign of her past lunch time. Yu Manli did not keep her appointment. As time went by, Ah-Xing's mood sank progressively from one of hope to disappointment, then despair, and finally to self-reproach. He blamed himself for misconstruing her gesture, for indulging his wishful thinking. Most probably he was never in Yu Manli's thoughts. Why else would she have broken the appointment with such nonchalance? Or maybe Yu Manli had come to regret her impetuosity and felt so ashamed that she never wanted to see him or visit the Heart Light Massage Center again. It was she who had fired the first volley and now it was she who beat a retreat. What was she thinking? He suddenly felt insulted and his inner pride swelled. He said to himself bitterly: "So you are not coming. That's fine. Nobody is begging you to come."

As he said this under his breath, Ah-Xing tried to keep the bitterness in check. Like a jilted woman who congratulated herself on not having lost her virginity to the jilter, he kept telling himself: "Luckily we only held hands, and for no more than ten seconds. Thank heavens we did not go further than that."

But there was no denying that Ah-Xing felt hurt. The injury was not very serious; it was an ache that soon turned into self-pity. That evening he decided to forgo supper. He went home, closed the door and did his penance alone.

When Chen jia meimei—a plastic bag of freshly cooked *zongzi*, with their bamboo leaf-wrapped sticky rice, in one hand and a pot of piping hot chicken soup in the other—kicked open the door to Ah-Xing's apartment, she found him lying in the dark. She cried with alarm: "Hey, Ah-Xing, how can you stay in the dark? Turn on the light now and have some of the *zongzi* and chicken soup I brought you. Mom made them. They are really delicious."

Whether the light was on or off meant little to Ah-Xing, but he flipped on the light for Chen jia meimei, who reversed roles by turning herself into the hostess of the household. She put the food on the table, dragged Ah-Xing toward it, and sat him down. Then she peeled a *zongzi* before thrusting it at his mouth, exhorting: "Eat it! It's stuffed with pork. It tastes real good."

The sticky rice with the tantalizing smell of pork was next to his lips. Ah-Xing was left with no choice but to open his mouth and take a bite of the *zongzi* held in Chen jia meimei's hand.

"Ah-Xing, it tastes good, doesn't it?"

Chewing the *zongzi*, Ah-Xing nodded. Then a strong, pungent current of air shot up his nose, almost bringing tears to his eyes. He quickly snatched the *zongzi* from Chen jia meimei and started to scarf it down. Chen jia meimei was mesmerized as she watched. She said approvingly: "Ah-Xing, you eat like a big tiger. Two bites and it is gone. You have such a big appetite!"

Ah-Xing was famished. He had forgone supper to punish himself for being thwarted in love. But how could he consider himself so? Yu Manli had simply decided to interrupt her back treatment. She was free to stop coming to Heart Light. It was silly of him to go on a hunger strike because of her. His self-reproach now took on a sense of guilt toward Chen jia meimei. The one who rejected his affection did it so ruthlessly, while Chen jia meimei was so full of natural goodness.

When Ah-Xing finished one *zongzi*, Chen jia meimei would peel another one for him. When he choked on the sticky stuff, she fetched the pot of chicken soup and thrust the ladle into his hand. As Ah-Xing slurped the thick, tasty chicken soup and ate the delicious *zongzi*, he thought that Chen jia meimei's niceness to him was something that was real, something he could hold on to, and therefore he should be nicer to her in return. With that thought, he said: "Meimei, I'll see you home tonight and I'll buy you ten mutton shish kebabs. What do you say?"

Chen jia meimei jumped with joy: "That's lovely. Let's go now!"

Without waiting for Ah-Xing to finish the rest of the soup, she grabbed his hand and dragged him toward the door.

That's how easy it was to make Chen jia meimei happy.

Ah-Xing was never one to have high expectations or great pretensions. It was not in his character to be overly romantic. It was just not in his blood. And as his life settled again into a routine, his mind became occupied with mundane matters. Gradually Yu Manli receded from the front stage to the back of his mind, in the limbo of half reality and half fantasy. When he occasionally thought of her, he felt only a vague regret.

But exactly two weeks after the Wednesday of her missed appointment, Yu Manli reappeared at the center. Just when Ah-Xing was on the point of forgetting her, she walked into Room 03 of Heart Light to the beat of Bach's minuet. The calmed waters of Ah-Xing's heart were once again churning. But he did his best to settle his wildly beating heart and speak to his customer as a professional masseur: "How are you, Manli?"

Yu Manli reciprocated the greetings as she went through the familiar ritual of kicking off her slippers and lowering herself on the massage bed. Ah-Xing reached out with his hands and once again came into contact with that smooth, satiny skin. And everything rushed back.

"Ah-Xing, how many weeks have I missed?" Yu Manli, her face buried in the hollow in the bed, asked in a muffled voice.

"How many weeks? Probably three, I think." Ah-Xing wanted very much to ask her why she stayed away so long. He was even more anxious to know if she'd forgotten how she had grabbed his hand in the last session and held it in hers for so long. He didn't have to, for Yu Manli mentioned it herself: "Ah-Xing, do you know why I did not come for three weeks?"

Ah-Xing answered truthfully: "No."

After a light-hearted laugh, Yu Manli abruptly turned over and sat up. She said, grasping his hand: "Ah-Xing, I can't tell you why just yet, but I will when the time comes. I want it to be a pleasant surprise for you. Just wait. A month from now, I'm going to tell you everything."

Ah-Xing could clearly sense Yu Manli's breath just inches away. He felt if he were to lean slightly forward, his face would touch hers. But he couldn't detect her usual scent of roses; there was instead an odd medicinal smell.

Letting go of Ah-Xing's hand, Yu Manli resumed her recumbent position, and with a muffled voice said: "Ah-Xing, meeting you is the luckiest thing in my life…"

The residual warmth left by Yu Manli on his hand triggered a burning, searing pain in his heart, a pain so intense he almost lost his head. Ah-Xing drew a deep breath and then another to calm himself before resuming his massage of her back. But his hands seemed to have lost their touch, applying pressure randomly and obviously absent-mindedly. Ah-Xing rarely got distracted when massaging his clients, but this time his attention strayed despite himself because he was parsing Yu Manli's every word and expression. She said she wanted it to be a pleasant surprise for him; she said meeting him was the luckiest thing for her. So what kind of pleasant surprise had she prepared for him? Ah-Xing dared not pursue the thought. This Yu Manli was nothing if not a siren who was trying to capture his mind and soul.

Haphazardly Ah-Xing rubbed and kneaded spots on Yu Manli's back. When his hand moved close to her neck, Yu Manli reached up and grabbed it. "Ah-Xing, don't massage my neck."

"Why?"

"I fell the other day and broke my jaw. The stitches were removed recently and it still hurts when touched." It all made sense now, Ah-Xing thought, that medicinal smell. "How did you fall? You've got to be more careful."

Yu Manli said with a laugh: "It was my carelessness. Don't worry."

An hour and a half later, Ah-Xing finished the massage. Yu Manli got to her feet and bade him goodbye, saying: "Ah-Xing, thank you very much! I'm leaving now and won't be back for a while. So see you next month at the usual time."

Ah-Xing was on the point of answering when he felt a pat, light as a caress, on his right shoulder.

"Ah-Xing, a seam on the shoulder of your white robe has burst open."

With that she said goodbye and exited the room. Ah-Xing listened for the slippers that tapped out a minuet growing fainter. He put up a hand to touch the spot on his shoulder where Yu Manli had just tapped him. It was true. A seam had opened a crack about one centimeter long. In his daily work as a masseur he moved his arms and shoulders a lot and that was where his robe was apt to rip.

Ah-Xing stood in the massage room, his left hand resting on his right shoulder. He could feel a burning sensation coursing from the shoulder straight to his heart. Yu Manli had touched him on more than one spot now, he thought, but today's touch was different from the previous one. He couldn't seem to put his finger on exactly what the difference was. He had been through some emotional ups and downs so he believed he was more sophisticated now. But some questions still puzzled him, like this one: what kind of pleasant surprise was Yu Manli planning to spring on him?

XII   The Beautiful Ugly Doll

After Yu Manli's departure, Ah-Mei came in to give Ah-Xing the latest news: "Xiao Lin said that Yu Manli was wearing a huge pair of sunglasses today, and so much of her head was wrapped in layers of gauze that Xiao Lin didn't recognize her at first when she came in. It was only when the invoice was written up that she found out it was Yu Manli. Why did she dress like that?"

"How should I know?"

After some consideration, Ah-Mei ventured a guess: "Did she cover her face up in shame because she overheard us calling her Peking Man?"

"That's not likely. When I was rubbing her back, she cautioned me not to touch her neck. She said she broke her jaw in a fall and needed a few stitches."

The mystery was solved for Ah-Mei: "Oh, she had a face injury. No wonder she covered her face. But why should it matter? Even without the injury her face has nothing to recommend it."

When Ah-Mei said this, she seemed to have completely forgotten that her own burned face was wrinkled like orange peel. Maybe she considered herself a beauty all along.

The inner battles in Ah-Xing's heart had now reached fever pitch. He had never expected his situation to be so complicated. In his present state of mind, life was like a voluminous tome, of which he had read only a few pages. Before he could read through the whole volume, he thought, he would already be dead. Yet there was so much in this book that intrigued him, so he felt compelled to read on even if it meant expending time and energy, even if the reading brought sadness, doubts, pain and tears.

Ah-Xing believed he could find everyone he knew—his elder brother, his sister-in-law, Ah-Mei, Yu Manli, Xiao Lin, Granny Yan, the chairman of the neighborhood committee and so on—in this book. Of course they were assigned different weights. Only a few pages would be devoted to Chen jia meimei, for example, and these would be an easy read, even a fun read. But it would be so banal it would hardly leave an imprint in the reader's mind. What about Yu Manli? She would be a harder read. This difficulty would pique the interest and curiosity all the more, and induce the reader to make a greater effort. When one tries harder, one makes an emotional investment. So Yu Manli would rate several chapters in the book.

With Yu Manli's reappearance, the inner calm that Ah-Xing had at long last managed to restore was once again shattered. It had been a difficult month, a month in which Ah-Xing found to his dismay a diminished sensitivity in his touch and his hearing. He used to pride himself on his ability to focus his mind in a way that was impossible for seeing people. He also had the skill of walking without the aid of eyes. His devotion to work was absolute. When he ate, he savored the food like a gourmet. He was able to turn the melody of music into his own language.

But now he got easily distracted by trivial things and frivolous thoughts. One day he even failed to sense imminent rain and neglected to take his umbrella with him when he left for work. And on another day he strayed from the blind path and walked straight into a shed for bicycle parking on the sidewalk. What took the cake was when he was massaging a client's knuckles and paused for a good ten seconds holding the client's hand until it was jerked free in protest, shaking him out of his reverie. He was lucky the customer was an elderly man.

Chen jia meimei visited Ah-Xing at home nearly every day. She always brought some food prepared by Chen jia muma. She told him: "Mom normally doesn't allow me go out and play. But if I say I'm visiting Ah-Xing, she always gives the green light."

It turned out Chen jia meimei was using Ah-Xing as an excuse to go out and have some fun. This girl of twenty-odd years did not treat dating as a romantic adventure but as something that brought certain benefits and privileges, such as a chance get out of the house, to have a change of scene, and of course, to snack on forbidden treats. Those were the incentives that kept up her enthusiasm for the game.

As for Ah-Xing, he indulged her because of some sense of guilt toward her. As long as he harbored any thoughts about Yu Manli, he felt an obligation to be even nicer to Chen jia meimei. But much as he pampered her, or allowed her the liberty of planting loud, smacking kisses on his face, he never had an urge to touch her, to put his arm around her, hold her, fondle her or kiss her back. Not at all, never. He felt that to touch her would be like child molestation and that would burden him with an even more guilty conscience.

Luckily Chen jia meimei's demands on Ah-Xing were limited to the supply of snacks and listening to her rave about Andy Lau. Ah-Xing found that there was even a utilitarian side to his own attitude: by being extra nice to Chen jia meimei while he awaited the pleasant surprise from Yu Manli, he would feel less guilty if he eventually had to break off with her. The thought make him shudder: didn't that mean Chen jia meimei would be the sacrificial lamb in this whole matter? He swore to himself that whatever happened he would be nice to Chen jia meimei, even if only as a sister.

One month had seemed like a long time but it

went by quite quickly. Ah-Xing counted the days and before he knew it, the day of the pleasant surprise was already upon him. Just past ten in the morning, the minuet footsteps echoed in the corridor and Ah-Xing's heart began to thump wildly. The footsteps came closer and the door to Room 03 was pushed open. Ah-Mei greeted her in a loud, clear voice: "Manli, how are you!"

Ah-Mei went out and closed the door behind her. Then, then...Ah-Xing stood where he was, as if he didn't know his place was on the high stool at the head of the massage bed. He stood as if in a daze until he felt a sudden pounding on his shoulder, followed by Yu Manli's voice, which sounded almost like a cheer: "Ah-Xing! I told you I would bring you a pleasant surprise. Here I come!"

Ah-Xing remained standing straight as a ramrod, his rigid body trembling a little. Yu Manli almost had her arm wrapped around his shoulder: "Ah-Xing, come, put out your hand and touch my face."

Ah-Xing was puzzled: "Your face? I've touched

it before. It is very beautiful."

Yu Manli laughed: "Yes, Ah-Xing, you were the first person in this world to say I was beautiful. You gave me confidence and courage. Before that, I would never have dared imagine I could be beautiful. I didn't even have the courage to go into a beauty parlor. But now, Ah-Xing, come. Come touch my face!"

Yu Manli grabbed his hands and raised them slowly toward her upturned face. Ah-Xing's hands now covered it entirely.

Whose face was this? Ah-Xing's hands froze as soon as they came into contact with her skin. Then he heard Yu Manli speak very close to him in a voice bursting with excitement, happiness and contentment: "Ah-Xing, if you could see, you would say now I am truly beautiful."

Ah-Xing's hands moved slowly, hesitatingly over the face. The skin, the muscles and the bones bore no resemblance to what he remembered of Yu Manli. It was not that extraordinary face that reminded one of the grassland music played on a horse-head fiddle.

Instead he discovered a face that was so ordinary, so plain, so without distinction. An uninteresting face indistinguishable from most other faces.

How could this be Yu Manli's face? Ah-Xing heard a pounding in his ears. What she was saying didn't seem to register in his mind although he was listening. His senses had stopped working! All he knew was his hands were feeling the face of a stranger, who kept pressing him: "Ah-Xing, tell me, is my face beautiful? Tell me!"

Ah-Xing's hands rested on her face, but he was unable to say the words expected of him: "Manli, you have such a beautiful face!" He couldn't bring himself to utter a sentence as simple as that.

He didn't know how long it was—it might have only been moment or it could be a long interval—before he gradually emerged from his daze and woke to the pain in his heart. He understood now that the woman he likened to a purple rose was gone. She was here to bid him goodbye. Her rambling voice was close to his ears; it sounded like a love story, something about an ugly duckling searching for love. Because of the praise and encouragement of a blind swan, that woman who called herself an ugly duckling became convinced she could become a white swan. The ugly duckling began to take action. The day the ugly duckling was to become beautiful finally arrived. And in order to show gratitude to the blind swan, she presented her own pleasant surprise as a gift, giving him the honor of being the first person to experience her new face. Then she went away with that beautiful face to look for the white swan of her dreams.

Ah-Xing still did not say the words that he had once blurted out to Yu Manli and that she expected to hear. Instead his hands said what he truly thought, but Yu Manli didn't comprehend. Maybe she was a little disappointed, however what mattered to her was not Ah-Xing's approval but her new-found confidence and courage to find her white swan. Ah-Xing had only been a catalyst for her.

Ah-Xing sat for a long while in Room 03, lost in thought and confusion. Now he could no longer think of Yu Manli as a purple rose. What was her color? It was elusive, indefinable.

An excited Ah-Mei burst into the room: "Ah-Xing, Yu Manli had plastic surgery! Xiao Lin said Peking Man is now a beauty."

Ah-Xing felt a tingling in his gums and then in his jaw. Ah-Mei continued: "Xiao Lin said nowadays you can have your forehead lifted, your nose sculpted, your cheek bones and jawbone reshaped. You could also have your skin tucked, your..."

During Ah-Mei's long soliloquy, Ah-Xing got to his feet. "I'm taking the afternoon off."

With that, he walked out of Room 03, out of Heart Light and straight into the sunshine. In that moment Ah-Xing felt a shudder rippling through his body, followed by a heartache that, like pulverized ice, cascaded from his blind eyes down his cheeks.

After he went home, Ah-Xing got in bed. In a state between sleep and wakefulness he was obsessed by a question: why was it that what he thought was beautiful was not beautiful in others' eyes? Even Yu Manli negated his sincere praise by having surgery. Ah-Xing discovered in the end, to his own astonishment, that he was beginning to have doubts about the judgment of his hands, skin, hearing and other senses.

Ah-Xing was heartbroken. He fumbled for the ugly doll lying by his bed. He had dumped it there and had not touched it again since he brought it home. He picked it up carefully and felt its grotesque yet lovely, plump face. Unaccountably he found himself missing Chen jia meimei very, very much.

Toward evening she arrived, bringing him a thick syrupy soup of tree ear mushrooms and lotus seeds. Ah-Xing got out of bed to open the door for her. Before she could put down the thermos containing the soup, Ah-Xing put out his hands and said with urgency in his voice: "Meimei, come over here."

Then Ah-Xing pulled her, together with the thermos, into his arms.

He thought, only Chen jia meimei, who was doomed to never grow up, would, like him, consider an ugly doll to have the most beautiful face in the world.

Keening

I

If you are not a native, you probably have no idea what *kuge* is. It is keening, a combination of wailing and singing where the wailing is embedded in the singing and vice versa—a harmonious integration and a perfect amalgam of the two.

In the small town of Liuwan, there is a mourning tradition passed down for generations among the female members of the family. At the funeral, they remember the deceased by reciting, through keening, notable events from the different stages of the person's life, his way of dealing with others, lifetime achievements, the ups and downs of the family's fortune. But this "wailing" is not like the wailing you may know; it carries a tune and therefore requires a good voice, a bright and clear tone, and a precision in hitting the right notes.

On top of that, it has to tell stories. After all, as critical as it is for the deceased on judgment day, how can the keener not try her best to include all the good deeds of the departed? The recitation needs to be delivered with colors and nuances. To tell a good story, one also needs to ad-lib and to render the mundane into memorable lyrics.

Keening tends to be long in duration. An untrained voice will become hoarse pretty quickly, and if so, the timbre, the precision and the volume will inevitably be affected. Therefore, a strong voice becomes very important for the family of the deceased.

You must understand by now that keening is something that requires special techniques and abilities, and it is considered by the townspeople of Liuwan to be a true "craft."

The popular saying that one can excel in any one of the "three hundred and sixty-five trades" finds its corroboration in the town of Liuwan. Take Young Bu in the bamboo business for example. He is so skilled at weaving delicate and exquisite bamboo baskets and containers that these everyday products have become upscale handicrafts doing good business in faraway U.S. and Canadian markets. By perfecting the craftsmanship passed down from his ancestors and expanding his sales overseas, Young Bu has become the indisputable leader in bamboo wares.

Another example is the good old lady of the Lin family who is known far and wide for making a special spongy sticky rice cake. When festivals approach, people from neighboring townships flock to Liuwan to buy her cakes, and they have to place their orders ahead of time or go back empty-handed. And so, it goes without saying that the good old lady of the Lin family has becomes the unchallenged number one in her particular field.

While such top-notch professionals in trades in Liuwan are few and far between, they are all true number ones: no cheating or funny business. They have earned their status through persistent hard work.

And so we also have a "number one keener,"

Xiao Fengxian. With a name literally meaning "little legendary phoenix," she was named after the famous courtesan befriended by General Cai, a hero who fought for China's transformation from the feudal Qing Dynasty into a republic. She has now earned the honor of being the top keener after having performed countless wailing songs at funerals, but like everyone, she had to start somewhere.

A while back, as a result of an official ban on any activity that smacked of "idealism," the craft of keening, which had been passed down for centuries, was almost lost. Few came close to even half mastering the art.

Recently however, seemingly out of nowhere, huge funeral processions have once again become the rage. And keening, as part of the funeral requirement, has also made a comeback, becoming a booming business. The only problem is: how can you find a keener among the younger generation of today?

They can cry for sure. How can they not shed

some tears over a deceased member of the family? Most of them make a nonsensical wailing sound with their faces smeared with tears and running noses. The most one can make out would be the words, "Oh, Dad..." or "Oh, Mom..." while the rest is totally lost to the audience. With such a lousy performance, how can you expect the deceased to be satisfied and leave for paradise voluntarily? And how can you make the living understand what a distinguished and brilliant life the deceased led, so that they will have an example to follow, and can convert their sorrows to strength and continue on?

When the matriarch of the Bu family died, Young Bu, the bamboo tycoon, found himself stymied by the difficulty of finding a good keener. According to ancient tradition, the louder the keening and the longer it lasts at the funeral, the greater the credit earned by the younger generations for their filial piety. If there is no one to keen, it is a sure sign that filial duty has not been satisfactorily fulfilled.

One could usually find one or two distant female

relatives to somehow do the job; they might not be all that good but they would be at least passable. But Young Bu and his wife were both born and bred in the new society. They belong to a generation that grew up under the red banner of socialism and they of course know nothing about keening. And certainly a funeral for the family dominating the local bamboo business would require a keener of superb quality and unquestionable skills. But how could one find such a person in today's Liuwan?

This added worry made Young Bu's slight frame even slighter and his pale face shriveled by anxiety, thin as an unharvested reed left standing in a pond. But however burdened he was, he still needed to find a keener for the funeral. His mother could then go to heaven accompanied by mellow and meandering singing that lamented her and told her story. As a pious son, how could he leave any impression to the contrary?

The suggestion then came that if no good keener could be found even among the distant female relatives, how about a substitute keener?

Those who were against the idea questioned whether anyone would agree to cry for another family's deceased. Wouldn't it bring bad luck to the keener's family? The proponent immediately came to his own defense, noting that what would make or break this case was money. If you were willing to put up the money, do you really think that no one would be willing to cry on your family's behalf?

What Young Bu was least afraid of was putting up the money. His bamboo baskets and chairs sold well, even internationally, and he had money to spare. Young Bu, dressed in mourning clothes and a white waistband, instantly took out a stack of bills from the sales of his bamboo products. In a voice that was not loud, but was clear and determined, he said: "I need help finding a substitute keener, and I am willing to pay two hundred per hour!"

The others started calculating right away. On the day of the funeral, keening must be performed for all groups of mourners, up until the time of the funeral procession. All told it would last at least six or seven hours—my goodness, over a thousand for a day's work? That is manna from heaven! But even with such high pay offered, it would still be difficult to find a keener who was not only willing but also of high quality. Could anyone really fit the bill?

The stack of money that had been slammed on the table by Young Bu remained there with no taker. As the ceiling fan whirred overhead, Young Bu's white linen mourning robe seemed to do a joyous dance and the bills were agitated to the point of threatening to fly apart.

In a corner of the living room, Young Bu's mother, whose breath stopped exactly 24 hours ago, lay covered by a white sheet. Vibrant colored plastic flowers stuck out from the bed frame, and the bed was ringed by large crystal-clear ice blocks that had been hauled from the ice house and placed on the ground. It gave the impression that Mother Bu was lying in a crystal casket decorated with fresh flowers. But the ice blocks were irreversibly melting and puddles of water already appeared here and there. The mourning hall was now suffused with the smell of incense and candles and the creeping cold air, but Mother Bu had died in high summer, and if she was not cremated by tomorrow, her body would start to smell. Young Bu was so desperately anxious that two blisters appeared suddenly at the corner of his lips.

Tang Guilong, a retired language teacher at the Liuwan Middle School, had been asked by Young Bu to write some memorial couplets for the funeral. Now, seeing how desperate Young Bu was, he knitted his eyebrows and racked his brain in search of a solution. After a long while, a former student of his finally came to mind. After graduation from high school, this student worked at the county Cultural Station and had been often seen in performances in villages and factories some time ago. Teacher Tang said: "This young lady was just wonderfully perfect in singing the opera highlight 'Baoyu by the Bier' from the famous 'Dreams of the Red Chamber.' From a soft cry in the opening phrase: 'Sister Lin, I am coming too late, too late,' she gradually transitioned to loud laments of anguish and grief, conveying an overwhelming sense of tragedy. As to her voice, its ability to move from high to low with ease, build up to a crescendo, and conjure a deep sense of loss and grief, never failed to move her audience to the brink of tears."

Tang Guilong was after all a language teacher, and the sophisticated words he used in his vivid description immediately convinced everyone around that the young lady must be perfect. Young Bu got so excited that he grabbed the weasel-hair writing brush from Teacher Tang's hand, exclaiming: "Thank heaven and earth, we finally found someone. Teacher Tang, please go and ask her right away. Money is no object as long as she agrees to come."

At the time, Liuwan was already under the jurisdiction of the Pudong Development Zone, one of the newest parts of the Shanghai metropolis. While Liuwan might be considered an exurb by some, with the skyscrapers of Pudong in front, the international airport in back, and silver-colored airplanes crisscrossing overhead, the townspeople considered themselves very up-to-date and worldly.

Still, every small town inevitably has its own

quirks and hangs onto its own traditions. In the matter of funerals, the townspeople of Liuwan simply refused to skimp. They were ready to break with all the other old traditions but adamantly refused to tweak the rituals concerning the deceased. It would be simply unconscionable to try to be frugal regarding the dead. In the eyes of the townspeople in Liuwan, the deceased is the one who calls the shots.

Even with this heavy responsibility thrust upon him, Teacher Tang left in full confidence. Hours later, he returned to the living room filled with wreaths and offerings for the Bu family. With him was the "young lady" who sang the famous highlight, the aforementioned Xiao Fengxian.

In fact, Xiao Fengxian had long passed the stage of being a young lady. She was now the wife of Yao Chunfu, a worker at the punching workshop of a hardware factory in Liuwan, and the mother of Yao Yao, a tenth-grade boy at the Liuwan Middle School.

Although Xiao Fengxian now stood in front of the Bu family, the road there had not been so smooth. At first, Xiao Fengxian would not agree to follow Teacher Tang to keen at the funeral. She said: "I can't cry for another family. It would bring bad luck. If my husband finds out he will give me hell."

Teacher Tang tried to make her change her mind: "We live in a new age now and should do away with such superstitions. Young Bu is willing to pay a very high price and here you are sitting at home and doing nothing anyway. Why pass up such good business? It could earn you over a thousand in one day. Once your husband knows that you are making good money out there, surely he is not going to blame you."

It was true that the price promised by Young Bu was very attractive, but keening is not opera singing. Xiao Fengxian tried to refuse the offer on that ground: "Only people of the older generation know how to keen. I don't."

Teacher Tang said: "While working for the Cultural Station didn't you sing in the Shanghai opera 'Baoyu by the Bier' and reduce all the women in the audience to tears? And bring the men to the verge of tears? Keening is quite similar to singing the part of Baoyu. You were so good then, how could your claim of not knowing how to keen be true? I know you can do it."

The minute that Teacher Tang mentioned the past, Xiao Fengxian became a bit dazed. Flashbacks flicked through her mind's eye one by one: bits and pieces of music played by a combination of string and percussion instruments, pretty faces wearing heavy makeup, and jerrybuilt stages made of wood planks. It all happened twenty years ago, well in the past now. But those were the days of Xiao Fengxian's pride—and the source of her pain.

II

Xiao Fengxian is not her real name, so what is it then? The townspeople of Liuwan had never wanted to pry.

It all went back to a song. At a joint party held by the teachers and students of the Liuwan Middle

School and the military forces stationed there, a female student had sung a theme song from a famous movie. In the movie, which depicted the love affair between Xiao Fengxian and General Cai, the female lead sang: "The mountain is blue, the water is green, streams flow from high mountains in rhythmic surges, in plaintive wails, in grief," lamenting how hard it is to meet a real friend, how hard it is to find a bosom companion. As the student sang this song, her voice was reminiscent of Li Guyi, one of the most famous singers of the time.

The soldiers in the audience listened to her with rapt attention, then clapped enthusiastically, loudly clamoring for an encore. What the soldiers were especially good at was tenacity. They chanted in unison: "One two three, better be quick. Four five six, get your picks. One two three four five, will you ever arrive? One two three four five six seven, Xiao Fengxian's voice is from heaven." Since the dear friend of General Cai was named Xiao Fengxian, that was what the soldiers called the student singer. And the name had stuck ever since that evening.

After graduating from high school she didn't do well enough on the entrance examination to get into university. Those were the years when the rate of admission was well below that of today, and there were as yet no private universities that would admit students as long as they could afford it. If your scores weren't high enough, you just had to go back to where you came from. But Xiao Fengxian didn't go back to her village. Thanks to her voice, she was recruited by the town's Cultural Station and became a performing artist.

As an artist with no regularly scheduled performances, she had to work at the town embroidery factory as well as in the field during harvesting and planting. Only when celebrating on special government occasions—the convening of some plenary session of the party's central committee or during some weeklong family planning campaign—would the performing artists be released from the embroidery factory for rehearsal.

The meeting room of the Cultural Station served as the rehearsal space for everyone, singers as well as musicians playing the flute, *erhu*, *pipa* or dulcimer. They would stage whatever programs they were asked to. It might be it a song-and-tale skit in the comic Shanghai *shuochang* style entitled "Joyously Greeting the Convening of the 13th Party Plenary." Or it might be the Songhu opera aria "Abida's Home Visit" or an "Autumn Harvest" dance, followed by street performances in heavy makeup.

At the time, Xiao Fengxian was considered a minor star in Liuwan. Her nickname, Xiao Fengxian, sounded like a screen name, and being referred to that way somehow had furthered her ambition for stardom. When a young woman suddenly finds herself becoming a star in a small town, she starts entertaining dreams beyond others' wildest imagination. Xiao Fengxian's dream was to become a real star.

She went to study with Fang Yaxin, a famous opera singer of the Xu School style who was part of the county's Shanghai opera troupe. The bulk of her wages earned at the embroidery factory went toward the tuition. But she learned all the roles so well that she could fool people into thinking she was a direct descendant and private pupil of Xu Yulan, the founder of the Xu School. "Baoyu by the Bier" was the jewel in the crown of her repertoire, and her performance of it was regularly scheduled by the Cultural Station.

Xiao Fengxian was running hard on the road toward fame. She wanted to be a professional performer, not a part-time one who had to work in an embroidery factory or in the field. For the county opera competition, she practiced hard and poured her whole heart into her performance. Her hard work was not in vain, as she won first prize. She was then recommended by the county to compete at the city level, where she won second prize.

She was at the threshold of becoming a real star, and the people of Liuwan treated her like one already. Devoted fans followed her everywhere she went spreading the word: "Xiao Fengxian is going to sing Baoyu." Other programs were her lead-ins. What was she if not a star in the eyes of the townspeople? Who would know what a real star should look like anyway? Xiao Fengxian didn't think much about all that. What she cared about was to squeeze through the narrow gate to superstardom. That was her dream, or should we call it her goal?

If things had continued on the way they were going, Xiao Fengxian might really have become a big star. If not a superstar, she could have become a leading local star, like her teacher Fang Yaxin, by joining the county opera troupe. If worst came to worst, she could at least have become a formal member of the town's Cultural Station and remained a performing artist.

But Xiao Fengxian was living during a period of rapid and momentous changes that leave those who fail to keep up in the lurch. These were the years when color television became a household item. Townspeople were able to watch the New Year's party aired by the Central Television Station as well as the major singing competition held in Shanghai. They came to know real stars: Mao Amin, the mainland singer with her signature "Nostalgia";

Tan Yonglin, the Hong Kong singer of "Love in Late Autumn"; and Qi Qin, the Taiwanese singer famous for his "Northern Wolf."

Once they had seen the televised performances of these superstars, the townspeople no longer cared much about what the county opera group would present. The Baoyu piece offered by their local star lost its shine. The programs of the local Cultural Station no longer seemed to satisfy the increasingly sophisticated level of appreciation of the population of Liuwan. Event organizers started inviting professional players from cosmopolitan Shanghai to appear. Big stars would come where the money was, and this was how the townspeople satisfied their growing taste for superstars. And how they were mobbed when they visited!

Like potatoes and turnips, the local stars would no longer suffice, and were soon reduced to has-beens. When the most famous Shanghai opera star Qian Huili came to Liuwan to perform the Baoyu piece, Xiao Fengxian was in the audience too. Once she attended this performance she realized that she couldn't hold a candle to the big star. It was not that the star's voice was far superior; it was the inexplicable factor that came from her style, her presence, her hand gestures and her movement. The townspeople of Liuwan knew an outstanding performance when they saw one, and they showered her with prolonged applause afterward. Xiao Fengxian was applauding too, joining the chorus asking for encores. But after clapping and cheering she was also jolted and shaken by a strong sense of loss. How could she describe the sensation? There was a tiredness around her jaws and a dull pain in her heart. Her dreams were so far away. They were shattered.

Some time afterward, the county opera troupe was disbanded. Its star, Fang Yaxin, bade farewell to the stage and became the owner of a clothing store. And what about Xiao Fengxian? Since there was no more demand for performances, her title of "performing artist" was no longer valid. That meant she would stay in the factory permanently as an embroiderer.

Her ambition in the years she was striving for

stardom had made it difficult to find a boyfriend locally who would be a good match. In fact matchmakers rarely volunteered their service, and the few matchmaking attempts all ended in failure. The men were always looking for a wife, and how could an actress be a good housewife? After several unsuccessful tries, Xiao Fengxian was considered someone who had passed her prime as a marriage prospect.

Although a woman above the usual age of marriage as well as a has-been star, she was still idolized by some. Among the young men who had adored her and followed her everywhere, there was one who harbored an abiding and unwavering love for her. Yao Chunfu, also considered over the age of marriage, was employed at the punching workshop of a hardware plant. A simple and timid soul, he became the earthling who asked for the hand of the fairy princess. And the fairy princess, who was savvy enough to know that her position and status were not what they used to be, agreed to this marriage proposal and descended to earth. In the twenty years since then Xiao Fengxian never sang again.

So when Teacher Tang arrived at her home and mentioned the Baoyu piece, she almost froze. When was the last time she sang? She had forgotten that she once was a performing artist. In her previous life, opera singing was her source of nourishment. She had spent days and nights studying voice, mastering the diction, the acting, the movement, humming tunes whenever she had a needle and thread in her hands.

It slowly came back to her that she had once had a dream, or even a goal. And now, the goal that had been buried deep inside was like a little snake opening its eyes after long hibernation, moving its body and ramming into the mud that blocked its exit. Nothing could have stopped its action, and the ramming caused ache and pain in Xiao Fengxian's heart. The little snake was about to emerge from the hole, inching its way through the tight seal that she had put there.

Xiao Fengxian just stood there in a daze. Teacher Tang sensed that she was about to make a move but was still hesitating. When one is unable to make up one's mind, sometimes all that is needed is a hint or a push by someone else to clear the head, get out of the quandary, and take a new step. Although Teacher Tang was now retired, for decades he had been the one who provided his students with the hint or push they needed. And so, while Xiao Fengxian was still lost in her stupor, he took her hand and dragged her out the door.

On the way to the Bu family's house, Xiao Fengxian seemed a bit confused. She appeared to have returned to a time many years ago. She was working at the embroidery factory one day when she was informed that they needed to work out a program that would be performed by the townspeople to entertain county government officials after they finished their tour of inspection. She dropped her embroidery work half-finished and hurried immediately to the Cultural Station. Large fields of golden rape seed flowers went by as did the sandstone pavement under her feet. She passed the closely packed houses along both sides heading toward the Cultural Station at the end of East Market Street.

Rehearsing was much easier than doing needlework all day. The satisfaction one got from the roaring approval of the audience was simply overwhelming, something that could be the cause of envy or even resentment among the townspeople. What would be on the program? "Baoyu by the Bier" was a must. Xiao Fengxian was a performer, and a performer always wanted to have his or her masterpiece included in the program.

At this thought, her pace seemed to have gained in speed and bounce, and her face became moist as if covered in beads of excitement. Good, she had finally arrived at the Cultural Station. The place was colorful, crowded with people, and it was permeated with the smell of burning incense and candles. Sounds of wailing could also be heard intermittently. "Oh no," she thought, "this is not the Cultural Station. It is the parlor of the Bu family home." The myriad colors came from the wreaths and offerings. The crowds were members and relatives of the Bu family. The wailing went on for a while and then was halted by others who offered comforting words.

Xiao Fengxian came to her senses slowly, finally understanding that she had followed Teacher Tang to where the Bu family was in mourning. She was not here for a rehearsal, she was here to keen. What should she do? She wanted to bolt for the door but Teacher Tang behind her whispered: "Since you are already here, why don't you give it a try, as a show of courtesy to your old teacher."

Xiao Fengxian didn't dare run away. She had come so far, she couldn't go back. Besides, Teacher Tang still respected her and considered her his student. How could she not return the courtesy? She would give it a try. There was really no other way out.

III

The next day, Xiao Fengxian donned a somber-colored dress, and with tears streaming down her face, keened five sessions spanning a whole day. But she had not been born with the skill, and really didn't do that well and wasn't convincing at the very beginning.

At first she stood in a state of high vigilance in the hall of mourning, where around the funeral bier, a new batch of ice blocks had just replaced the old ones. Her nose wrinkled at the trace of bad odor in the cold air. When the first group of mourners arrived, Young Bu pointed out to her in a whisper: they are the nieces and nephews of my mother. Xiao Fengxian nodded, calmed down and was ready to start. But this whole thing seemed so strange. Why was she here to cry for others? Keening was not like singing on stage, and she had a hard time assuming her new role.

If Xiao Fengxian found it difficult to step into her new role, the mourners were somewhat at a loss too. Several young people just stood around the bier and didn't know what to do. The scene was a little too quiet. People in the hall started talking in a low voice as they waited for Xiao Fengxian to open her mouth. They became impatient and started fidgeting and chitchatting; what was this hired keener waiting for?

It was at that moment when Xiao Fengxian was nudged by someone from behind and stepped forward almost involuntarily. The nudge could have come from Young Bu, his wife, or even Teacher Tang. She had no choice now but to brace herself for the task at hand. Xiao Fengxian took a deep breath, closed her eyes and opened her mouth. A quivering and plaintive voice that marked the beginning of the keening cut through the mourning hall filled with people: "My dear flesh and blood..."

The cry immediately stopped all noises and the hall was in dead silence. Where was she? She opened her eyes in great dread and saw only wisps of incense and the flickering candles. Faces passed by in a flash, their eyes focused on the keener in great expectation. Just like many, many years ago, when she was surrounded by people coming to see her performance in a village, she was on stage, and the words she memorized were about to come out. She collected her thoughts, touched the bier and uttered sotto voce: "Sister Lin, I come too late." The second phrase followed, cried out in a heartbroken lament: "I come too late..."

The wailing, which conveyed so much grief and pain, woke heaven and earth, opened up the listeners' pores, and elicited wretched sadness in their hearts. Wasn't this quiet hall a stage? And wasn't the phrase "my dear flesh and blood" a lead into what is to follow? Her sealed-off memory suddenly became wide open. She was indeed singing "Baoyu by the Bier." There were so many people watching, it was time to start singing. The lead-in was over, which meant she should now sing in free style, senza misura. Slowly and wistfully she sang the lament: "My dear flesh and blood—you departed in such a hurry, leaving us with immense sadness. My dear flesh and blood—you can no longer respond to my call, leaving us heartbroken..."

Who was the deceased on view? That was no longer important. What was important now was the fact that Xiao Fengxian was playing the role of a keener. There were so many people in the audience, so many onlookers—what was it if not a performance? But it was also true that she was not surrounded by fresh flowers and applause, but rather by funereal wreaths of all sizes, and the family members of the deceased in mourning clothes. Was the Xiao Fengxian who sang "Baoyu by the Bier" the same one who now wailed on behalf of others? Since when had she been reduced to a keener? Was she at long last closer to her aspiration or farther away from it?

Her tears simply gushed out uncontrollably. She cried real tears to her heart's content. She was no longer crying for the deceased lying among the ice blocks. She was crying for herself, for the realization that the flower of her once beautiful life was now withered, and for the reunion of her live body and her long dead soul. She looked miserable in her bitter lamentations, tears streaming down her face, her wailing heartbreaking. Everybody was affected and started sniffling. Those nieces and nephews who had been unable to get in the mood were now were calling out with tears in their eyes: "Oh, auntie, auntie!" With everyone in the hall crying, it was a scene of sadness and grief.

When the first session of keening for Mother Bu came to an end, everyone agreed that this professional keener had a supple voice that traveled far. But as a first timer who had no past experience whatsoever, she had let herself become overwhelmed by grief and missed the essence of keening. Her singing lacked variety; she overplayed the grief part but was a little short in modulation and elegance. The content of her keening was also too narrow; she certainly conveyed the sense of loss but not much about the lifetime achievements of the deceased.

Xiao Fengxian cried so hard that after the first group of mourners departed, she was still standing there sobbing. Young Bu came in and handed her a bottle, saying: "Have some water."

Xiao Fengxian took the bottle, her shoulders still shaking from overwhelming grief. Young Bu advised: "If you keep on like this, you might die from exhaustion before anyone could figure out what you were trying to say. We just had the first batch of mourners. How can you last a whole day?"

Her shoulders stopped shaking right away and the sobbing sound originating from deep in her throat also disappeared. She could tell that Young Bu was letting her know that she hadn't done a good enough job and that the mourners couldn't make out her words. She realized she was there to keen for others and not to lament her own frustration or misfortune, and that her crying so hard would not be appreciated. She made some swift adjustments to her mindset. She needed to save her energy. She just did one session so far, and would need to assume different characters for the second and third sessions. She needed to adapt to her role and not mix it up with her own life.

This is the difference between keening and singing. In an opera, the performer and the role need to be totally integrated. But the requirement for keening is that one has to go into and come out of different personas. Once you can do that with ease you can be called a true professional.

By the time the second batch of mourners came in, Xiao Fengxian had learned her lesson. She reminded herself to rein in her emotions and give more thought to tunes and lyrics. Indeed she made progress the second time, and every time afterward. By the last session before the funeral procession, her progress was virtually measured in leaps and bounds. She was keening on behalf of Young Bu and his wife, the deceased's son and daughter-in-law. With the lessons learned in the previous rounds, the lyrics she made up on the spot were very much to the point. She betrayed just enough emotion and the modulated tone was touching as well.

Her singing, time and again, took the listeners back to the hardships Mother Bu went through while bringing up her children. The half-an-hour long keening session just before the procession had started the gathering crowd—the neighbors and relatives of the Bu family—weeping in grief. Young Bu and his wife were down on their knees, choking on tears. Xiao Fengxian's keening, with its expressive melody and clearly enunciated lyrics, was interspersed with the couple's sobbing cries. The mixture seemed to have an especially tragic effect. In the end, it was Xiao Fengxian's keening that pushed Mother Bu's funeral to a climax.

Xiao Fengxian's very first attempt at keening on another's behalf had concluded with resounding success. She won high praise from all the funeral guests: she was so wonderful; her skills so solid; the voice so perfect; the story line so clear. To Xiao Fengxian's surprise, she was somewhat pleased with herself as well. It was much like in the old days, when she couldn't help but feel proud of herself after receiving resounding applause and bravos for her performances. The sense of accomplishment that had been missing in her life for so long had returned unexpectedly today.

There was a traditional tofu banquet, showing thanks to those who had contributed in cash or in kind to the funeral, to mark the funeral's end. After the guests departed, Young Bu took out a stack of money and gave it to Xiao Fengxian, who still had red eyes and a dizzy head from too much crying, telling her: "You worked very hard today and this is your remuneration."

The hand that received the money betrayed some hesitancy. Xiao Fengxian blushed, as if to convey that taking the money was not entirely appropriate. Young Bu, who never found himself at a loss of words, came to her rescue, saying: "Take it, you've earned it. And I hope you won't find it ungenerous of us."

These words finally persuaded Xiao Fengxian to take the money. But weighing it in her hand, she felt that it was a little too heavy. She blushed in embarrassment again and stammered: "Boss Bu, this is too much."

Young Bu dismissed her protest with a wave of his hand. "You keened so well, very much to the point. You deserve it all, and we might need your service..."

He had been about to say: "We might need your service in the future." But he stopped short when he realized that both of his parents were now gone, so if Xiao Fengxian's service was ever needed again, it would be on the occasion of his or his wife's demise. He would then be making a reservation for Xiao Fengxian to keen for one of their future funerals. These words would bring bad luck to the family. After all, how could anyone want to make a reservation in this kind of business?

So Young Bu pulled the brake in the middle of that sentence, and immediately changed tack. "In this day and age of 'reform and opening up,' there is nothing unseemly in someone getting paid for her keening service. Is what you do in anyway different from me weaving bamboo ware or the good old lady of the Lin family making sticky rice cakes? Our labor provides us with a livelihood. Keening requires talent; you cannot be a good keener without the requisite skills. Moreover, releasing the souls of the dead is considered a virtuous good deed. If there are other families who need a keener, I will recommend you. This is the way things are done. There is no need to feel embarrassed."

Young Bu was a person who was able to make

a convincing case for anything using a few verbal acrobatics, thanks to his experience and worldliness. With the stack of money clutched in her hands and the words of Young Bu in her head, Xiao Fengxian's thoughts ran far afield.

IV

By the time Xiao Fengxian reached home, it was already evening. Although her eyes were red and swollen, her steps were exceptionally light and bouncy. Yao Chunfu was having a dinner of rice porridge and a dish of salted vegetables. His face was livid and his features twisted. Their son Yao Yao was watching television in another room, mimicking at the top of his lungs some singer from Hong Kong or Taiwan: "I cannot afford to lose you, Annie. I can't forget you, Annie. With my life I am calling to you and will love you always..." He had inherited his good voice from Xiao Fengxian, and now as a teenager, his voice change was almost complete.

Seeing Xiao Fengxian's return in the corner of his eye, Yao Chunfu didn't acknowledge her. Holding the rice bowl in hand, he continued eating, making all kinds of noises. The singing and the music from the other room seemed to have gained in volume now. Without any provocation, Yao Chunfu suddenly slammed the rice bowl hard on the table, and the clash of the ceramic bowl with the table made a loud thud. The porridge inside splashed all over the place. The bowl miraculously remained intact, but the same couldn't be said of Yao Chunfu. So loud that he risked tearing his vocal cords, he roared: "Stop wailing like a mourner! I will give you a good smack in the face if you keep on doing it!"

The singing in the other room stopped abruptly. Xiao Fengxian knew Yao Chunfu must have heard that she went out and keened for others, and he was just trying to provoke her by pretending to scold their son. She hurried to the table, started cleaning up the spill, and said in an apologetic tone: "Chunfu, do you know how much I made today?"

Yao Chunfu twisted his lips a little and didn't respond. He wouldn't dignify the question with an answer, thinking that even if you could make three or five hundred a day as a keener, it is still a disgraceful profession. Xiao Fengxian wiped her hands clean, took out the stack of money from her pocket, and said with a smile: "I made sixteen hundred."

Yao Chunfu was flabbergasted. After a while he finally recovered and said: "What kind of world are we living in today? You can make more money in one day of crying than I can working for a month."

In spite of her red and swollen eyes, Xiao Fengxian's voice remained bright and clear: "They are willing to pay me a good price because, first of all, they have money; and secondly, I am a good singer."

In making that statement she betrayed a sense of smugness as she beamed with satisfaction. She was indeed endowed with a good voice, and one that didn't get hoarse even after crying a whole day. Yao Chunfu was in a quandary. The sixteen hundred yuan had indeed doused his anger. But this was, in the end, money made by his wife for mourning for others, a job he didn't consider to be half decent. He accepted the money handed to him by Xiao Fengxian and sighed wistfully: "Tell me, how do you expect me to hold my head high in front of people if my wife goes out and mourns the dead of other families?"

Yao Chunfu apparently could no longer be mad at what she did, in light of the sixteen hundred yuan, but he wasn't ready to admit defeat either. He felt the need to make a statement. His statement couldn't be too strong though, because he already had the money in his hands. And yet, his statement couldn't be too weak either. That would mean his slamming of the rice bowl on the table and his shouting of threatening words at his son would have been just a show. Under the circumstances, the most appropriate thing seemed to be to express a kind of helplessness. What can you do? She had been there and made the money. She certainly couldn't be barred from coming back home. And what would be the point of throwing away good money?

Many years ago, when Yao Chunfu and Xiao Fengxian were newlyweds, he truly treated her as a princess. He loved her and cherished her and supported her financially. But after having to deal with the mundane matters of daily existence by himself for a while, he came to realize that marrying a has-been star actually made no practical sense at all. He would have fared much better if he had found someone more skilled at household chores. What good was an opera singer? In bed, with the lights off and your eyes closed, it made no difference.

After the embroidery plant closed its doors, Xiao Fengxian couldn't find another job and stayed home cooking and washing for her husband and son. The family budget was especially tight because of it. In the blue sky above her head she could see huge silvery "birds" leaving the international airport for destinations all over the world, and yet she hadn't even been to Beijing. There had been no improvement in their material life nor had their spiritual life been any better. She hadn't sung any operas, not to mention joining the latest rage of karaoke or ballroom dancing. In short, her family was not doing particularly well in these new categories of "civilization."

No one addressed her by the name Xiao Fengxian anymore; in Liuwan she was referred to as the mother of Yao Yao. When the Shanghai opera "Dreams in the Red Chamber" was shown on television, Xiao Fengxian would immediately switch channels. She couldn't bear to see others singing the "Baoyu by the Bier" highlight. It was like a dead body that couldn't bear the sight of its surviving soul. The soul was making the dramatic gestures, the soul was delivering the lines, and the soul was singing the operatic lyrics. That soul had long left its dead body behind and they could no longer be reunited.

Only Xiao Fengxian knew that kind of sorrow. And that is why she was determined not to see that particular highlight on TV. But Yao Chunfu was as fascinated by the Shanghai opera as always. He would stare at the screen and say: "Who could have believed that this was once in your repertoire when you were young? If not for your singing of this piece, we would not have been what we are today, and Yao Yao would not have been born."

Xiao Fengxian would argue with herself: "Would we be what we are today if I had made it in the opera world? Yao Yao wouldn't be called Yao Yao, he would have a different surname." Of course, she didn't say these words out loud, but she felt suffocated, as if she had a growth that interfered with her breathing. She would step away from the TV and retire to the bedroom. As for Yao Chunfu, with no one there to grab his remote, he just relaxed in front of the television and watched other people singing "Baoyu."

Xiao Fengxian then realized that her husband married her because he was in love with the role she played in the opera. After living with her, in the flesh, day in and day out, he no longer treasured her as a rare find, and had instead gotten nasty and impatient with her. The more she pursued this line of thinking, the more upset she became. But all she could do was lament: "I can't even hold onto the job of an embroiderer, so I have no one to blame but myself."

But today, on her way back from the Bu family, her mood was decidedly different. Maybe it was the result of a good cry that washed away all the sludge and debris that had made her feel suffocated. With the blockage gone, the almost forgotten feelings of satisfaction and accomplishment were making a comeback. She had to admit that she enjoyed being surrounded by people, being the center of attention, being a star. She didn't even care that much about the stack of money from Young Bu. She took the money home to placate her husband, because the satisfaction and exhilaration she got from doing the job were of no use to him. In that sense, money was an "extra" that Xiao Fengxian got for her keening, much like a free gift that came with a purchase. Of course, she had handed over that free gift to her husband.

As expected, Yao Chunfu was thrown by the sixteen hundred yuan he didn't work for, and he didn't know whether to blame Xiao Fengxian or not. He just sighed time and again before putting the money in his pocket and retiring for the night with yet another sigh. But this proved to be a sleepless night for Xiao Fengxian. No matter how hard she tried, and how much she tossed and turned in bed, her mind was unstoppable: the singing and the music, the scenes, on and off, up and down the stage, from the past to the present. Her eyelids were still puffy when she got up the next morning, but she seemed to be in exceptionally high spirits. After serving breakfast to her husband and son, who then left for work and school, she locked up and made her way toward East Market Street.

She now missed the rehearsing and performing days at the Cultural Station long ago. When had she last set foot in that place with which she was once so familiar? She was like an abandoned child who had long wandered away and had almost forgotten what her parents looked like. She hated the parents for abandoning her and had chosen to stay away, pointedly avoiding any mention or discussion of them. It was not that the child didn't miss her parents, but she wanted so much to make it on her own that she simply couldn't untie the knot in her heart by forgiving her parents. And so, in the eyes of others, she seemed like such a heartless child.

Xiao Fengxian was that abandoned child and the Cultural Station her unlucky parents. But the child inevitably would miss her parents one day. And yesterday's keening at the funeral finally crumbled Xiao Fengxian's last resistance. She felt like making the trip to East Market Street to see the parents with whom she had lost touch for so many, many years.

The Cultural Station was still at its old place at the end of the street. The minute Xiao Fengxian appeared at the door, the room darkened. The place looked deserted except for a young man playing cards there. Without raising his head, he asked: "What are you here for? Are you looking for someone?" Xiao Fengxian couldn't say if she was looking for anyone; she was there only to take a look at the place where she had once lived and worked. Or, you could say that she was there to visit the self that had died. Since she now felt she was alive again, she must have made it back to this world through reincarnation.

This place with which she was once so familiar—the ferry she had fervently hoped would deliver her safely to the other shore—looked so dilapidated. The paint on the desks was peeling, the cabinets against the wall were missing either doors or drawer knobs, and the ceiling fan blades were covered with a thick layer of dust. It was a dingy place, and the air was stuffy and musty. It seems that while everything else in the world has changed, the Cultural Station alone had stopped where it was twenty years ago. Looking at the sorry state the place was in, Xiao Fengxian felt a tingling in her nose and her eyes welled up.

The card game the young man was playing wasn't going anywhere, so he threw the cards down and stood up. Finding Xiao Fengxian still at the door, he said: "Gee, how come you're still here? Is anything the matter?"

Xiao Fengxian replied with a smile: "No, nothing is the matter. I was just looking around. Young man, is the meeting room in the back still there?"

The young man said: "Yes, but it was rented out a long time ago. It is an Internet café now."

Xiao Fengxian felt somewhat lost, and then the shiny bald head of the director of the Cultural Station, Qiu Yinsheng, came to mind. "What about Master Qiu? Is he still around?"

Master Qiu was an expert on folk art and an important member of the performing group. He could play the trumpet and the two-stringed fiddle, the *erhu*. He composed songs too. Then a man in his thirties, already with a glittering head, he was the one who took the young men and women on performing tours through the countryside. His head became the sun for Xiao Fengxian and the others, and they would follow that sun anywhere. Master Qiu had gone bald prematurely, and everybody said then that he looked like an artist. But twenty years down the road, it seemed his shiny head had failed to turn him into a real artist. The office of the Cultural Station looked to Xiao Fengxian's eyes more like a trash collection station.

The young man, who had started his card game

anew, replied: "Master Qiu? Are you talking about Qiu Yinsheng? He quit the post a long time ago."

Xiao Fengxian stared ahead blankly. So Master Qiu also left the Cultural Station. On second thought, that was also understandable. How many among the singers and performers of those days didn't change their profession? The young man once again lowered his head and shifted all his attention to the apparent suspense and dire challenges of the card game at hand. Xiao Fengxian felt dismissed and was ready to leave. But before she turned around, she couldn't help asking another question: "Where is Master Qiu now?"

The young man flipped the cards and sounded somewhat impatient: "Qiu Yinsheng has formed a band and is in the funeral music business. The whole world knows that! How could you not know?"

Leaving the Cultural Station, she was hit with waves of emotion—anguish mixed with some consolation. Master Qiu's funeral music business and her keening service were similar in nature; you could even say that they were in the same trade. She began to feel some additional compassion for the shiny bald head in her memory. Apparently Xiao Fengxian was not the only one who had abandoned her ambition. Who could have thought that time would fly so fast? That things would change so dramatically? That they would both be involved in the business of releasing the souls of the dead from purgatory? Stirred by her conflicting emotions, she once again couldn't stop the tears from coming to her eyes.

V

Ever since she keened at the funeral of Mother Bu, Xiao Fengxian discovered that the funeral business was thriving in Liuwan. In the remaining two months of summer, she got two more customers through Young Bu's referrals. And then people began to ask directly for her services, without going through Young Bu.

Now she would no longer cry her heart out and get entirely exhausted like she did the first time.

Now her keening skills were much more proficient, and she could go in and out of the role at a moment's notice and with ease. Her style grew out of "Baoyu by the Bier"—fiery sentiment tempered with tenderness, and sadness mixed with nostalgia. She was able to move everyone in the audience to tears while eliciting feelings of respect, love and fond memory for the deceased.

Her mourning could be considered both a literary and a musical achievement. In no time, Xiao Fengxian had become the most talked about highlight of the funerals in the area. Naturally the fee associated with her first-class keening performance was considerable, but the families concerned would always oblige, lest they be accused of being ungrateful to their elders and become pariahs in their community.

When Xiao Fengxian accepted her payment, it was always preceded by a show of declining to take the fee, as if to make the point that she was not doing it for the money. But why do it if not for the money? She hadn't really given much thought to this question. Maybe deep in her heart she equated her work as a keener with her previous opera singing career. The fact that she was making good money was something she didn't plan for. Her performances in the past had always been for free, but nowadays no one expected stars to perform without payment.

The oldest person in Liuwan died in the winter right after her one hundred and fourth birthday. She had been regarded as the "living treasure" of the town, and at her death, government officials, the street unit, her offspring, relatives and neighbors showed up in full force to mourn. For such an important occasion, which was to be attended by high officials, the service of Xiao Fengxian was of course required. In addition, monks were asked to recite sutras and an ensemble of Chinese wind and percussion instruments was also invited.

When someone dies at a very old age, their funeral is considered a celebratory occasion as well, and with so many performances, it can look more like a performing arts show. And it was at the funeral of this centenarian that Xiao Fengxian came across Master Qiu, standing among other members of the ensemble with his trumpet in hand, blowing hard from inflated cheeks. Master Qiu had only been bald at the center spot back then, with sparse hair remaining on the edges. But now that barren terrain had expanded to include his whole head— he had no hair whatsoever left. She also recognized several other members of the band who, like her, had all been recruited as performing artists in the past by Master Qiu. Carrying their instruments and stage sets, they had been her constant companions during their performing tours in the countryside many years ago.

Xiao Fengxian and Master Qiu only had the time to briefly acknowledge each other's presence; no words were exchanged before they had to take their respective positions. While Master Qiu was no longer the master of the Cultural Station but rather the conductor of a small ensemble, a cultured quality still seemed to exude from his every pore.

As different groups of mourners arrived, he

would give quick instructions to the players of the flute and the stringed *erhu* and *yueqin*, and then with a slight nod of his bald head as a signal, music would rise in the air. Xiao Fengxian waited until the guests were lined up before the bier, and as the instrumental music gradually came to an end, she opened her mouth and let her voice spiral up the scale. It was always Master Qiu who accompanied her singing of "Baoyu by the Bier" on the *erhu* back then, and their coordination even after a hiatus of almost twenty years was still quite good. With one out in the yard and the other right by the bier, they seemed to understand each other without the need for words. The music and the keening would rise up, each in turn, complementing and never interfering with one another.

There were simply too many people paying last respects to the centenarian, so Xiao Fengxian had to use a microphone, a wireless one at that. Out in the yard, two huge black amplifiers stood under the winter sun. The keening was carried far and wide via the sound system: it could be heard all along the street and even up at the next intersection. The sales clerks at the department store and hardware store, the waiters and waitresses, the customers at the restaurants and the tea houses, all were within the reach of the amplifier carrying the keening mixed in with music:

In spring when the willows were green,
Auntie was grinding the Mondo grass tuber,
With me weighing on her back,
She was unable to stand up straight,
Dear auntie;
In summer when lotus flowers perfumed the air,
Auntie held me sleeping in her arms,
Constantly waving the cattail leaf fan,
She shooed the mosquitoes away,
My dear relative;
In autumn when mums were in bloom,
As I learned to walk,
With her big hands,
Auntie held tight my fat little hands,
Dear auntie;

In winter when the snow flurries descended,

In freezing temperature,

Auntie washed my diapers,

Her hands got frostbite,

My dear relative!

This "Four Season Melody" was keened on behalf of the nieces and nephews. The touching story line was delivered with mournfully sweet vocals. The minute Xiao Fengxian opened her mouth, professional tears started streaming down her face. To her listeners, her singing and keening were so hauntingly beautiful and sad, they couldn't help but join in her sorrow and cry.

As her rendition came to an end, all the guests had nothing but high praise for her performance, agreeing that no one could come even close to her. As to Xiao Fengxian, she took out a handkerchief, and as she dabbed her eyes and face dry, she looked as calm as if she hadn't experienced anything out of the ordinary. She laid down the microphone, slipped out of the service hall before the next batch of guests arrived, and ran to where the music ensemble was stationed. With great excitement, she called out at the exceptionally shiny head: "Master Qiu, I haven't seen you for such a long time! How have you been?"

With a big grin on his face, Master Qiu immediately replied: "Not bad, not bad. I've known for quite some time now that you are a first-rate keener, very famous. But I never had the chance of appreciating it until today. You did very well, very well."

Other members of the ensemble chimed in: "You did an excellent job, Xiao Fengxian! We haven't seen you for a long time! You have just gotten better and better!"

Xiao Fengxian was a little embarrassed. To those familiar faces she responded with modesty: "It's very kind of you to say that. I didn't know what I was doing."

She again turned to Master Qiu: "Master Qiu, you would tell me where I didn't do well, wouldn't you?"

Master Qiu's answer sounded both polite and tactful: "You did nothing wrong, nothing. But there is room for improvement here and there. There are rules to follow even in keening. Let's see, when the funeral is over maybe I can find some time and explain the rules to you in detail."

Xiao Fengxian blushed a little. She had the urge to learn more, the same way she felt under the tutelage of Master Qiu in the old days. She agreed: "Okay, after this is over, in the afternoon, I will come looking for you instead of going back home. Thank you, Master Qiu."

Another batch of guests arrived, so Master Qiu turned toward the band members and said: "We are about to begin. Pay attention to the nod of my head." He then put his mouth to his trumpet, and with an incline of his bald head the music started. Xiao Fengxian hurried back to the service hall and grabbed the microphone. Minutes later, the music drew to a close and the heart wrenching keening rose up again. This time, she was singing a "Song of Filial Piety" on behalf of the grieving grandchildren:

Dearest Grandma!
We light a bunch of incense,
With both hands, we stick it in the burner,
And pray that your soul will linger,
Dear Grandma!
We light three sheets of paper money,
As they burn into ashes and embers,
You, we will always remember.

The amplifiers carried the keening loud and clear to the yard outside. A thought went through Master Qiu's mind while listening to it: "Xiao Fengxian really has potential. She has talent. How could you let a talent like that go to waste?"

The funeral concluded as a great success, and the host was generous with the fees as well. After receiving the payment, Master Qiu dispensed the money among members of the ensemble so that they could all go home. Xiao Fengxian got her fee from the host too. Putting the money in her pocket, she waited for Master Qiu at the side of the yard. The winter sun set early, and at four in the afternoon it was already waning. Like tepid bath water, its warmth dissipated quickly with each wind gust. With his neck half hidden and his hands in sleeves, Master Qiu walked toward Xiao Fengxian, saying apologetically: "Sorry to have kept you waiting."

Xiao Fengxian replied without any hesitation: "Since I'm the one who will benefit from your teaching, waiting on my part is entirely proper."

Master Qiu said: "We need to find a quiet place to talk. We can't do it standing around like this."

Xiao Fengxian couldn't think of any place that might be appropriate. After searching his brain for an answer, Master Qiu said: "If you don't mind, why don't you follow me to our practice room. It's a sparsely furnished place that used to be the warehouse of the embroidery factory. When the factory closed, it became unoccupied, and now I rent it as our practice room. It's cold but spacious."

Xiao Fengxian replied: "That sounds good. Anyway it is better than staying outside in the wind."

Ignoring the curious looks cast their way by

passersby, they walked out of the courtyard of the centenarian and toward the factory at the edge of the town. Although they had lost touch for almost twenty years, now that they had run into each other, Xiao Fengxian again felt as excited and happy as she did years ago.

The man who now walked next to her still seemed to be the one she knew so well so long ago. There was no need for coyness or formalities. She felt that she could still jump up and playfully swipe her hand against his bald head, or insist on being treated to an expensive coconut ice cream at the end of a successful performance. She was in a good mood; in her eyes even the surrounding winter scenery exuded a warmer glow. The elm trees had shed all their leaves, but the bare branches seemed to exhibit the artistry of a bonsai plant. The wheat field at a distance was covered in splotchy brown mud, but the damp, cold air that she breathed in tasted like the coconut ice cream of Master Qiu's long-ago treat, sweet and soothingly cool.

The embroidery factory now came into view. It

was located at the edge of Liuwan Township, close to the countryside. The place was in disrepair: the factory walls had been dismantled with only piles of broken brick pieces left behind. It was surrounded by large patches of withered wild grass. Someone was lighting a fire to warm up cheap alcohol not far from here, and wisps of blue smoke rose up slowly against the setting sun, adding to the grayness of the sky.

Master Qiu took out a key and opened the worn-out wooden door to the small warehouse. Xiao Fengxian was right behind him and couldn't suppress her surprise: "Wow, this is really nice!"

Compared to the crumbling scene outside, the inside of the small warehouse was much better. The room was about fifty square meters in size. In the center, four classroom desks formed a large platform on which were scattered *erhu*s, flutes, gongs, small cymbals and other instruments. A dozen or so chairs with chipped paint were placed around the platform. Colorful silky gowns hung on the wall; they were not of high-quality material but the colors were vibrant. Master Qiu said: "Come in."

The room was too large and indeed sparsely furnished, and the minute she set foot in inside she felt a rush of cold air creeping up her spine. She shuddered but was excited nonetheless. The simply-furnished small warehouse looked very much like a practice room, and this brought her back to the meeting room at the Cultural Station in the early days. They both shared the same layout and atmosphere, and even the same old smell. She observed her surroundings in silence while combing through her tumultuous emotions. Master Qiu cleared his throat and said: "Let's begin now; we have no time to waste."

Xiao Fengxian immediately grabbed a chair and sat down. Master Qiu then started his lecturing: "The custom of keening has been in existence in our area for quite some time and it occupies an important place in Chinese folk culture. To be exact, the practice started under Emperor Wu in the Han Dynasty more than 2,000 years ago. There were famous funeral songs in ancient times; they are called keening songs locally, and are like elegies in literature."

Xiao Fengxian remembered Emperor Wu of the Han Dynasty from her high school history books, but she didn't know that keening started back then. She hadn't had the chance to learn her skills from any of the old keening masters. Now Master Qiu, by telling her the detailed history of this art form, acted as a teacher of sorts.

Master Qiu continued: "The most representative elegies are *Xielu* or 'The dew that on shallot-leaves lies' and *Haoli*, 'The grave site.' *Xielu* was sung at high society funerals while *Haoli* was meant for ordinary people. These two elegies, which were popular during the Western Han Dynasty, are the earliest recorded."

Xiao Fengxian was surprised that Master Qiu knew such a great deal about the history of keening. And she asked the question that immediately came to her mind: "Master Qiu, how did you come to know so much?"

Master Qiu answered with a smile: "As the activities of the Cultural Station dried up in the last few years, I organized the players from our old band to work at funerals. That's when I started reading books and did a little research."

Xiao Fengxian looked up at him, appearing more attentive than ever. Master Qiu took up an *erhu* and said: "Let's listen to *Xielu* first. The lyrics can be found in *Shijing, The Book of Songs*. I did the composition myself, amateurish as it may be, according to my understanding of the text." He then tuned the fiddle a bit, sat down, and put the *erhu* on his thigh. Raising his arm, he started moving the bow and sang the words, seemingly oblivious to his surroundings:

> How soon the sunlight dries
> The dew that on shallot-leaves lies
> Yet the same dew
> Though now 'tis dry
> Tomorrow morn will fall anew
> But when shall mortal men
> If once they die
> Ever return again?[1]

---

1   Translation by John A. Turner

The tune was totally new to Xiao Fengxian, and the lyrics, since they were in classical Chinese, were not easy to understand. She didn't quite get the full meaning, but the mournful singing of Master Qiu accompanied by the plaintive *erhu* sounded especially sorrowful with a sense of anguished beauty. Master Qiu's pale white face affected by wisps of melancholy now showed signs of age, but while caught up in singing, he radiated an aura of youthful bookishness.

After finishing *Xielu*, Master Qiu stopped the bow and explained: "As I mentioned, this work from the *Book of Songs* was sung at funerals for people of high status. Its tune is elegant and expresses a more controlled sense of grief. *Haoli* is different; it mourned the ordinary people, The sentiment it expresses is bolder and more direct." Master Qiu resumed his playing and sang:

The grave site
Whose site is it?
The site that collects the spirits of all

Good or bad
Wise or foolish
Why is the King of Hell so eager
Not allowing lives to linger

The two songs were clearly different. With the second, the style was more wretched and fiery. These two elegies were like the crying of two different women, one brought up in a well-to-do family and the other a simple peasant woman. One was suppressing her grief and the other was crying her heart out without inhibition. While Xiao Fengxian couldn't comprehend every word she understood the essence.

Master Qiu was absolutely devoted in his teaching. He played and he sang, catching her up in the mood, and she felt the natural urge to sing along with his *erhu*. Daylight was almost gone but they did not turn on the lights. Their continued practice in the dark seemed less a discussion of keening than a pretext for reliving the feelings that both had found hard to leave behind.

The air in the room was by now frigid. Master Qiu kept playing, his shiny head bobbing with emotion. Xiao Fengxian was standing nearby, paying the utmost attention to every word, every phrase, every pitch and every sound she uttered. They both appeared to have returned to the Cultural Station's meeting room of many years ago, to a time when they had to put in extra rehearsal for an upcoming performance, oblivious to hunger and the passing of the hours.

VI

By the time she arrived home it was past eight thirty. Yao Chunfu was still not home, most probably out playing mahjongg at the recreation center. Yao Yao was watching TV in the other room. It was an American on the small screen this time, who appeared to be a black man who had bleached his skin white. The American was not singing; screaming was more like it. And Yao Yao was screaming along enthusiastically with him. The house was a mess: bowls and plates were piled on the table, and clothing, shoes and socks were scattered everywhere. With a sigh, Xiao Fengxian started tidying up the place. While she busied herself getting things in order, her mind was back at the warehouse of the embroidery factory, and the lyrics and music of the elegies were at the ready in her throat.

Nowadays, Yao Chunfu no longer sighed time and again at the sight of Xiao Fengxian returning home from keening. In the past six months or so, he had reinvented himself using the money his wife brought home. His mode of transportation had been upgraded, the bicycle replaced by a brand-new light motorcycle whose speed and comfort his old bicycle simply couldn't match. He now had his own personal Nokia cell phone. He felt an ease, exchanging off-color jokes with his colleagues and friends during his free time. His life had all of a sudden become much more interesting.

He also bought Playboy brand leather shoes,

Montague T-shirts and a crocodile-skinned briefcase, all of which were brand-name products available only in the tax-free kiosks at the international airport several kilometers away. He now cruised to work at the hardware factory on his motorcycle with his cellphone in his pocket. He had to wear his uniform at work, those were the rules. But every Sunday, looking like a village entrepreneur in his brand-name outfits, Yao Chunfu would frequent the village recreation center and tea houses.

Even as he spent freely the money Xiao Fengxian made as a keener, he was becoming increasingly repulsed by her. Every time she came home from work, Yao Chunfu would blow his nose hard, as if she had somehow brought home the contagious air of the deceased from the funeral. "Go, go and wash yourself quickly. Go change your clothes right away. You are covered in the smell of incense and candles. It is disgusting."

Yao Chunfu looked more and more like a person of status. A thought crossed Xiao Fengxian's mind as she looked at this totally changed man: her husband did look handsome after all this sprucing up, which was something she never noticed before. It showed the difference that money could make. Although he was not the one who made the money, his appearance had changed dramatically for the better. Well, people do say that man is at his prime at forty, while a woman at forty is in decline.

At night, lying in bed, the one in decline tried to get the one in his prime interested. She tried flirting but he didn't respond. She tried to lure him with tenderness but he remained standoffish. She couldn't take it any more, flinging the comforter off, jumping up and saying: "Yao Chunfu, I am being nice to you. Don't take it for granted! Tell me, what did I do that you should treat me with such disdain?"

The one in his prime responded coolly, snubbing her: "It is not disdain. I just can't get used to the smell of burning incense that clings to you."

With these words, he turned around and went to sleep, his back toward her. It was a long and sleepless night, a night of immense sadness for the woman in decline. Tears rolled down her cheeks, wetting her pillow. But it didn't matter that her eyes would be all puffy the next day. Since she was in the business of keening, her eyes were always red and swollen.

The next night, Yao Chunfu didn't get back until after midnight. The minute he arrived home he went to the bedroom and picked up the coat Xiao Fengxian wore that day, putting his hand inside the pocket. Xiao Fengxian was not yet asleep. From beneath the comforter she told him: "I put the money in the drawer already."

Yao Chunfu immediately went to open the drawer of the cupboard by the bed and saw the rather thick stack of money. He put the money into his own pocket, and with a deep sigh he finally sat down and lit a cigarette. After a few puffs, he remarked to her where she lay under the covers: "God damn it, I lost so much money today! I couldn't find my way home, and I even had to give my cell phone up as collateral."

Xiao Fengxian sat up in horror. "What did you say? Didn't you promise you would just play for fun and never gamble?"

Blowing out a puff of smoke, Yao Chunfu defended himself: "How can you call this gambling? To real gamblers, this would be a pittance. You should give me credit for telling you the truth. At least I didn't lie to you."

Xiao Fengxian climbed out of bed, and without putting on an extra layer of clothing to fend off the cold, she confronted Yao Chunfu in only her thermal underwear. "That's because you had no choice. If you didn't have to get the money from me, you would lie through your teeth. Now give the money back to me."

Yao Chunfu pretended not to know what she was talking about: "What money?"

Xiao Fengxian, turning purple either from the frigid air or from anger, answered: "The money you just took from the drawer. Give it back to me."

Yao Chunfu made a few noises through his nose, scoffing since he felt he had a very strong case: "I need the money to get my cell phone back."

Xiao Fengxian immediately jumped to grab the coat pocket of Yao Chunfu, who at first tried to dodge her by holding tight to his pocket. But seeing that she had no intention of letting him off the hook, he didn't defend himself any more. With a ferocious expression, he grabbed her hand, but the words that came out of his mouth sounded more helpless than intimidating: "If you don't give me the money I will have nothing to give but my life to repay the debt. I might as well tell you now that I sold the motorcycle already. I'll have to steal and rob, and you won't be able to stop me."

Xiao Fengxian crumbled to the ground in utter frustration. Was this man her husband? She raised her eyes to look at the dejected face of Yao Chunfu, remembering the days of long ago. He used to follow her everywhere, showing up at all her performances in the countryside, and cheering for her when she entered the county-wide singing competition. He was so devoted to her and his feeling for her seemed so pure. As a fan, he was always faithfully by her side, and in the end he married her.

But now, how had he become what he was today? Did the money she made keening bring him to it? Or perhaps men who are opera fans and chase stars are by nature frivolous and up to no good. He didn't squander money then because he had no money. Once he had money his true self appeared. The more she thought about it, the sadder she became. She felt that this was her fate; she was doomed to marry a spendthrift. She loved opera singing too much to escape the fans or the misfortune they brought.

In the end, she didn't get her keening money back from Yao Chunfu's pocket. Minding his own business, he finally lay down in bed. As if afraid that she would grab her money after he went to sleep, he slept fully clothed with his hand holding tight to his pocket. Xiao Fengxian stayed on the ground for a long while, not feeling the cold although she had only a thin layer on. She wanted to have a good cry but couldn't; she felt so much hurt and sadness deep inside but the tears just wouldn't come.

Here she was, a woman whose profession was to cry for others, but when she herself was in grief, she found she was unable to cry. Did it mean that she also needed to find a stranger to cry for her when she felt sad and blue? She asked herself that question: "You are always crying for others. Is there someone who can cry for you?"

VII

Xiao Fengxian formally joined Master Qiu's group, which he had given the somber name of Funeral Service Corporation. Master Qiu was quite resourceful, and told Xiao Fengxian: "Working together is better than going it alone. Our band is in the business of providing a funeral service. You are a keener, so we are in the same line. Cooperation between two top performers is bound to be good for business."

Xiao Fengxian agreed completely with Master Qiu's idea, mainly because she felt that such a union would give her a sense of security, just like in the old days when she had the support of an organization. She had long been without a work unit. Although her keening business had been thriving in the past year, she never felt secure on her own. And once she joined Master Qiu's group, she would no longer fight her battles alone.

Master Qiu said: "Aside from providing instrumental music and keening, there are many other services we can provide: supplying equipment, arranging ceremony details and coordinating the burial."

Xiao Fengxian kept nodding her head like a chicken pecking at grains of rice. Not even in her dreams did she ever think that one day she would again follow Master Qiu, traveling to performances and busily building up her career. Master Qiu was truly someone who combined business talent with the spirit of reform. He pointed out: "To be true to our name as a corporation, we have to be able to provide first-rate service. The days of small-time are over—we now need rules, procedures and discipline. Of course, what is most important is to make sure our products are of top quality, or else we will be crushed by competition."

Xiao Fengxian was not very clear about what he meant by quality products, so she asked: "I thought we were providing funeral services. Are we producing goods on the side as well?"

Master Qiu laughed: "Services are counted as products, of course! For a keener like you, product quality depends on your performance. Now you no longer represent only yourself. The reputation of the whole company is on the line, so you have to make sure you are doing quality work."

After grasping the meaning of his words, Xiao Fengxian was like a race car with a full tank of gas, waiting for the starter's signal. "Master Qiu, can I get a few more lessons from you? As the only keener in the company, we can't afford a substandard performance on my part!"

Very satisfied with her positive attitude, Master Qiu remarked: "You're right. We now need to work out a keening program, and that requires our joint effort."

This is how the two of them worked things out, through rational discussions, moving beyond even

the model husband and wife who treat each other
with respect.

If keening was a folk art, and her appearance at
funerals a performance, then Xiao Fengxian could
definitely be considered a performing artist in hot
demand. And now that her business affected the
economic return of every individual in the company,
the driving force behind her performance was much
more than just her dedication to art. In order to
further upgrade her "product quality," and enhance
the reputation and earnings of the company, Xiao
Fengxian often stayed behind with Master Qiu in the
warehouse of the embroidery factory for additional
rehearsals. Master Qiu had an extraordinary depth
of knowledge and talent; he seemed to have endless
stories to tell and theories to explain.

They even went to the countryside together
to visit people who were too old to travel anymore,
collecting from them keening passages that were once
in vogue but had almost been lost. In Master Qiu's
notebook you could find research and phrases such
as "ad-lib keening," "restrictive keening," "thematic

keening," "hair combing song," "a daughter's tribute to her mother," "a song for funeral processions," and so on. It became a very thick book.

Thanks to Master Qiu's efforts in collection and synthesis, supplemented by Xiao Fengxian's assistance, they created through this new collaboration a set of specialized keening songs: for husbands, for children and for other relatives, and for themes such as "passing the bridge of no return" and others. To call it a true joint collaboration was to overstate Xiao Fengxian's role. Master Qiu was the driving force, and it was to him that most of the credit was due. It goes without saying that in the eyes of Xiao Fengxian, his stature and charisma were ever on the rise.

Xiao Fengxian had nothing but respect for this bald-headed man who had such an aura of culture about him. In fact, there seemed to be no connection between him and the funeral business. He should have been a scholar doing research in folk music, a restorer and champion of folk art. It was not enough to say she respected him; she now kind of worshiped and admired him as well. Perhaps she had never really figured out the distinction between respect, worship and admiration—all she cared about was that she liked his teaching, she liked to listen to him sing the funeral songs he had arranged accompanied by his own *erhu*, and she also liked to tag along on his many research trips to the countryside.

In short, with Master Qiu, Xiao Fengxian would forget that she was a keener. That aura she felt around him had proven to be very attractive to her. And through her proximity, she felt herself drawn closer to the temple of art and culture. She came to believe that keening was but an art form and the keener was the vehicle for that art. In Master Qiu's words: "You are not only keening for the deceased. You are using it to spread folk art and preserve our ethnic culture."

But this kind of total dedication by those in art, even to the point of being oblivious to their physical needs, turned out to be beyond the understanding of the townspeople. There had to be something going on between a man and a woman who spent so much time together. How could you explain it otherwise? Rumors started to fly.

One night, she came home and was surprised to find that Yao Chunfu wasn't out playing mahjongg as usual. Reclining in the newly bought rocking chair with a grim face and a fierce look, he stared at the woman who just stepped inside. Xiao Fengxian didn't feel like talking to him. After all, aside from the money in her pocket, in which part of her did he still have any interest? But he initiated a conversation: "I heard you are having a good time lately."

Xiao Fengxian felt a thump in her heart and retorted right away: "Talking about a good time, you're having a far better time than I am! You don't make money and yet you have plenty to spend. What a carefree life!"

This is how they clashed with each other, sparks flying in all directions the minute they started a conversation. The woman was formidable but the man was no push-over either: "Since you are helping the Casanova make a fortune, there should be nothing wrong in the cuckold husband enjoying some small change from that big pile."

She couldn't take this insult lying down. "Watch your words! Who has made you a cuckold?"

Yao Chunfu jumped from the rocker, saying: "You have the nerve to ask me to watch myself? The whole world knows that you and the bald guy have a suspicious relationship. What kind of fool do you take me for?"

Xiao Fengxian jumped even higher. "Don't you engage in pure fabrication and make unfounded charges against me! How dare you accuse me when you yourself are leading a corrupt and immoral life?"

He burst out laughing. "You see, even the words you use are different now: 'pure fabrication,' 'unfounded charges.' Where did you learn such fancy terms? From the Casanova? I am sure even your body smells like that pompous character!"

The woman flew into a rage. Like a small hen stung by a wasp, she flapped her wings and flew toward the man. With a clacking sound, the sound of skin clashing, the face of the man and the palm of the woman ran into each other violently. The sharp pain in her palm traveled all the way to her armpit. She had hit him too hard, way too hard. As to the man, his cheek immediately turned bright red. Stunned, he covered his mouth and stared at her with wounded eyes. He didn't seem to believe that she had just slapped him so hard. After quite a long time, he sputtered: "A woman who slaps a man will have bad luck. Just wait and see. Your luck will run out one day."

Xiao Fengxian's reaction had been a bit overboard. Her customary good manners were really just a front; she was actually a fiery-tempered woman inside. Her husband had thought he'd finally caught her in the wrong, and could use this to squeeze some more money out of her. It wasn't that he didn't care about the rumors, but there was nothing he could do about it. He was vulnerable in that he was incapable of making a lot money yet he spent money like water. This was his Achilles heel.

A kept man had no real voice and a man with no voice could only curse. Hence he cursed the woman who slapped her man. Yet he was also taking a risk in cursing her. If she really ran out of luck, who would support his mahjongg-playing and gambling habit? Yao Chunfu knew very clearly the importance of Xiao Fengxian, and refrained from challenging her ever since she slapped him. He went on with his life, working happily, coming home safely, playing mahjongg assiduously, and gambling seriously. His life was not at all empty; it was in fact a life full of excitement.

So Xiao Fengxian had apparently won this round of the match, but the victor still felt heart-broken. When she next had the chance to practice alone with Master Qiu, she poured her heart out to him. That evening, in the warehouse of the embroidery factory, Xiao Fengxian, in tears, told him the whole story of the fight she had with her husband. The one who did the talking was overwhelmed by sorrow and anger; the one who listened was trying hard to calm her down with kind and gentle words. In the end, extending his lean pale hand, Master Qiu patted her sobbing shoulders and remarked gravely, using a famous quote from the poet Bai Juyi of the Tang dynasty: "We both are strangers stranded in a foreign environment. Alas, aren't we all faced with the same situation?"

Xiao Fengxian didn't quite know what he meant by the quote, but she understood the latter part of his lament. Like her, Master Qiu must have also been confronted with the suspicion and challenges of his wife due to the rumored affair. He had been her spiritual anchor but at that moment she was somewhat confused. Why did she confess to him the sordid affairs of her own household? Why was it that as soon as she stood before him, she became someone overflowing with femininity and tenderness, someone without inhibition? Why was it that the hand touching her shoulder made her feel so warm, so disturbed that she was about to lose her self-control? Did it mean that all the rumors of an affair between her and Master Qiu were indeed in a way?

The more she tried to sort it out, the more confused and dazed she became. Her eyes, which had been staring at Master Qiu, became confused and evasive too. The hand on her shoulder lingered for a long time; it didn't seem to want to move away. Her heart, which had been broken in pieces just a while ago, now stirred up in light ripples like the surface of a pond after the soothing touch of a spring breeze.

Xiao Fengxian could sense a strange feeling rising up inside her. It was a feeling that Yao Chunfu hadn't caused in her ever since she became a professional keener. When was the last time she had had physical contact with a man's body? She almost forgot that as a woman she was entitled to personal pleasure too. At this moment she felt an urge, in body and mind, to enjoy such secret pleasure.

That evening, Xiao Fengxian and Master Qiu left the warehouse only after it became completely dark. With their actions, they turned the rumor into reality. Before departing, Master Qiu cautioned Xiao Fengxian with a serious expression on his face: "We have families and kids. We need to keep this to ourselves."

Xiao Fengxian replied: "I'm not a fool. Why would I speak to anyone about this?"

Master Qiu nodded and left the place first. Xiao Fengxian followed, watching his shiny bald head disappear into the night. This man, so strong and virile a while ago, now walked along with a light and soft gait. She couldn't but feel overwhelmed by a sudden surge of sweetness. She thought of how strongly the hands of this slim and gentle man had rubbed her breast, even to the point of being rude, hurting her. All men are the same; at critical moments they behave so differently to their usual selves.

That night, Xiao Fengxian was completely unable to fall asleep. The dull pain coming from her breast made her feel at once shameful and sweet. She was after all a traditional woman, and if Yao Chunfu was now someone she despised, he was her husband all the same. Even if they had to eat separately and sleep in different beds, she would not divorce him. As to Master Qiu, he had a wife and children too. It would also be impossible for him to go against custom and tradition. Given the situation, she could settle for having someone who truly loved her, and definitions were of no importance.

Ever since then, Xiao Fengxian had acted more generous and thoughtful. Resigning herself to the fact that she was married to someone who needed her support, she continued to give money from her keening to Yao Chunfu. Although he didn't fulfill any physical duties, she gave him money as if she was compensating him for being a cuckold. On the other hand, she also made a decision: she would set aside something for herself and no longer give all her earnings to her husband. She would be acting irresponsibly toward her future self and toward her son if she didn't save some money of her own.

VIII

Winter was over. Spring was in the air. The wind was no longer unbearably cold, and the willow trees sprouted yellowish green young leaves. The funeral company was doing so well that they had more business than they could handle. Xiao Fengxian's keening was the company's top product: it had won the most praise and was best-known. As a result her workload had become way too heavy, averaging several keening sessions a week. Although she now could recite both the lyrics and tunes by heart, keening was a mentally exhausting job. She had lost weight and looked tired as a result of her busy schedule.

Master Qiu said: "You work too hard. With so much demand, you can't handle it all. Let's recruit another keener." Xiao Fengxian was a little hesitant at first. With another keener in line, would her own position be jeopardized? It was like an opera troupe, where the star did not want to see his or her position threatened. Master Qiu, on the other hand, had the future of the business in mind, telling her: "For the company to sustain its growth, we need to strengthen the workforce and scale up. We also need to have sound rules and regulations in place. Once we hire a new recruit, you will be her teacher. Later on she will be able to take up some of your workload, so you won't have to work so hard any more."

Looking at things from this perspective, Xiao Fengxian realized that Master Qiu had a point. The advantages of having an apprentice would certainly outweigh the disadvantages. And with Master Qiu in charge, he would make sure that she was not shortchanged. They were now "wearing the same pants," to use the local expression, and were virtually inseparable. She was finally convinced by this line of reasoning, conceding: "It may be a good idea but where can we find our recruit?"

Master Qiu gave his luminous head a few strokes, his two eyes shining brightly: "At a family funeral at the Seashore Village some time ago, a young niece keening for her uncle did a decent job. She might be a good candidate."

Xiao Fengxian searched her memory but couldn't remember the niece at all. It must be that as a master of the art, she didn't really pay attention to the young girl, an amateur. Master Qiu was different. He always looked at things long term, considering their potential. That was how the niece came into his viewfinder.

Master Qiu recalled: "This young girl came to mourn her uncle but was snubbed by her aunt for some reason. The aunt would not recognize her as a relative and refused to give her the traditional white funeral clothes to wear. The girl then approached the bier and started her keening in full drama."

Xiao Fengxian asked: "What did she lament about?" Master Qiu replied: "I can't remember the lyrics entirely but they went something like this:

With you, dear uncle, on the road of no return,
How can your young niece carry on?
When you were alive, you took care of me,
Treated me, your niece, more like a child of your own.
In days ahead I am like floating duckweed,
No one to bother to pick me up,
No one I can count on.

Xiao Fengxian was completely surprised. How

did she not notice this girl who keened so well? Master Qiu, with a certain smugness on his face, added: "I asked around and learned that the young girl's name is Jiang Meihua. Wasn't that great?"

She nodded but her feelings were decidedly mixed, as if someone just upset the cruet bottles.

Now Xiao Fengxian had an apprentice, and she was the only one in the company who also doubled as a teacher. She was devoted to her teaching and her apprentice studied hard. In no time Jiang Meihua was able to take on keening performances and put all her learning to practice. The result wasn't bad but she was not yet half as good as her teacher. She sounded like Xiao Fengxian in form but not in spirit.

Xiao Fengxian often couldn't help but compare herself to Jiang Meihua since the comparison so far was still in her favor. Jiang Meihua had a good voice and was a solid keener, but she was not yet as cultivated and experienced. Jiang Meihua was young, had an innocent look, and had more physical endurance. But everyone was young once. When Xiao Fengxian first sang "Baoyu by the Bier," she was so young and beautiful, she almost became a star!

Age had caught up with Xiao Fengxian. Her physical condition was deteriorating, and now a session of keening often left her bone-tired and dizzy. Her voice had never gone hoarse before, but recently after keening for only half a session, her voice would become raspy. Plus, the arm with which she slapped Yao Chunfu six months ago had a dull pain ever since. The pain was not confined to her arm; when she pulled on her arm she could feel the gnawing and pricking pain extending to her armpit as well as her chest.

The pain in the arm could be explained by her slapping hard at her husband, but she didn't know what could have caused the chest pain. Was it somehow related to her arm? Or was it the result of the hard kneading by Master Qiu? But she had only slapped Yao Chunfu once, and ever since then her palm never again even touched the face of her husband. And Master Qiu didn't rub and pinch her breasts that often either. That only happened when they were in the mood and when opportunity allowed. And yet, her arm and chest were in constant pain, so something must be wrong. The words uttered by Yao Chunfu, his hand covering his red face, popped into her head: "A woman who slaps a man will have bad luck." Xiao Fengxian felt a little unsettled. She asked herself: "Is it possible that Yao Chunfu's curse has come true?" She decided to go to the hospital, alone.

At the village clinic in Liuwan, a dark-skinned, plump doctor with heavy eyebrows and large eyes extended her dark fat hand, reaching under Xiao Fengxian's clothing dexterously and pinching her hard on the right breast. Xiao Fengxian grimaced in pain. After withdrawing her hand, the gynecologist said with full confidence: "Yours is a serious case of lobular hyperplasia."

Xiao Fengxian didn't understand what lobular hyperplasia was. The doctor answered her question right away: "It's a hyperplasia, or abnormality, of the mammary glands. It's a common problem among middle-aged women, and is related to an abnormal ovarian function."

Xiao Fengxian still didn't really get it. "How can it be treated?"

The gynecologist suddenly furrowed her heavy brows and gave an evasive smile: "How can it be treated? Ask your husband to touch you more! Is it true that you don't make love as often anymore?"

Xiao Fengxian's whole face blushed in embarrassment. Not only did they not make love often, they had stopped altogether a long time ago. Of course, occasionally she was with Master Qiu, but only occasionally. It would therefore be entirely true to answer "yes" to the doctor's question.

Wiping away her evasive smile, the gynecologist resumed a serious look and advised her frankly: "Don't think as you grow older that you don't have needs. The best way to treat your disease is to have a harmonious and regular life as a couple."

But it was absolutely impossible for Xiao Fengxian to have "a harmonious and regular life as a couple." She didn't have that kind of desire for Yao Chunfu, and anyhow, a harmonious relationship was out of the question. Her relationship with Master

Qiu was harmonious but it couldn't become regular. He was not her husband so she couldn't possibly count on him to come to bed every night and create a "harmonious life."

The gynecologist's suggested treatment really left her in a quandary and it became a constant worry for her. Fortunately, the company was doing so well that even people from outside the county came seeking their service. Jiang Meihua's keening was improving, which proved to be a plus, not a minus, for Xiao Fengxian's reputation. Her fame grew even further for having such an excellent student. Master Qiu continued to be good to her, as he was in the past, and the largest share of the company's profit always went to her. These were happy things for her, and when she was happy, she forgot about her illness. She was doing well and life was looking good.

One day, the company was hired by someone from a neighboring county. They all boarded a bus sent by the family of the deceased and traveled for more than an hour. The band marched into the yard already playing, making quite a scene with all the pomp and circumstance. The members of the funeral service company were treated in the best way ever. Not only were they given first-class wine, cigarettes and meals, but Master Qiu was also treated with special respect.

As her eyes followed the enormous shimmering pearl of his head, as he busied himself here and there, Xiao Fengxian felt especially proud and happy. She was truly attracted to this extremely capable man. To an outsider it appeared that Master Qiu was the one who managed the business of the company, but in truth it was through their joint efforts that it had become what it was today. In fact, it wouldn't be far off to call it the "mom-and-pop" business of Xiao Fengxian and Qiu Yinsheng.

Embarrassed at this thought and the pleasant feeling it gave her, she blushed. Of course no one regarded the funeral service company as their "mom-and-pop" business. How could they be called a couple? No matter how widespread the rumor was, they were not a family. Although she stopped regarding Yao Chunfu as her husband a long time ago, he, not Qiu Yinsheng, was still her husband in the eyes of others.

Understanding this, she couldn't but feel somewhat lost. However, looking at the extravagance before her eyes and thinking of the high praise from the crowd, she realized she had reached a new level. The reception for her long-ago performances in the countryside had been nowhere near this scale. This fact alone filled her with gratitude to Master Qiu and gave her a sense of confidence. She figured that she was truly blessed. With all this real happiness and success, how could she ask for more in name? One should not be greedy or even God would not oblige.

After the funeral that day, the company was dutifully transported back to Liuwan by the host. After the members of the ensemble all went home, Xiao Fengxian stayed, inviting Master Qiu in a sweet and seductive tone: "Would you agree to go home a little later today?"

He replied: "Oh, I have some business to attend to at home. Next time, then."

Xiao Fengxian was upset and her eyes turned red. With a glimpse at her, Master Qiu said: "Okay, okay, I will go home a little later."

The two made themselves at home in the small warehouse of the embroidery plant. The ensemble no longer practiced here, and the room now served as the office of the Funeral Service Corporation. Master Qiu had it renovated after he formed the company. The walls were now covered in light yellow Nippon paint and the floor was laid with Marco Polo tiles. The row of cabinets against the wall was used for the storage of instruments and equipment, and two desks were set by the window, one for the company accountant and the other for Master Qiu.

The room became dark after Xiao Fengxian closed the door and the blinds. Master Qiu was sitting by his desk getting the scores in order. He said with his head down: "Hey, it is too dark, let's keep the lights on." But Xiao Fengxian didn't turn on the light. She walked behind him, holding him to her chest with both arms. With his bony back pressed against her, she could feel the pain stemming from her right side. The advice of the gynecologist came to her mind: the treatment of her problem required the massaging of the lumps and "a harmonious and regular life as a couple." Right now, she was hoping to enjoy with him some time as a couple, and he wanted to turn the light on! He was so bookish.

With her chin touching his bald head, she moved her lips and let out a giggle. The bald head of Master Qiu was getting itchy from the breath of the giggling Xiao Fengxian, and he tried to duck without success. She was holding him so tightly that he could feel her breasts pressing against his back. He was getting turned on by her teasing.

He was a man after all, and even a man with a slight build could have enormous strength at a time like this. He held both of her hands, turned around and immediately she fell into his arms. Xiao Fengxian's giggling turned louder. She deliberately arched back a little, and he wasted no time in lifting her up and laying her on the desk. She was now lying face up before him. Her eyes, burning with desire, glanced seductively at him as he busily took off his shirt and unbuttoned his fly. She was using her eyes to beckon him to caress her breast, to massage the lobular hyperplasia.

With her body stretched out and in full display, she was inviting him to come together with her as would a normal husband and wife. She needed this man, who could bring back her health, make her feel younger and more like a woman. And he, after shedding his armor, was ready to engage in a different battle. His hands immediately reached out for her chest, and he detected problems right away. His grip was forceful, and the minute he pressed with his palm he felt that something was wrong. The flesh was not as soft and supple as it was before; now he could feel that there were small knots underneath. Taking a quick look at the lump of flesh with its hard nodes, he discovered that the smooth and silky skin was now puckered like an orange rind. He lowered his head for a closer look, pinched the breast a little with his hand, straightened up, and with a grim face asked her: "What do you have here, breast nodules or ringworms? It's so ugly."

Leaving her lying face up on the desk, he turned around and began to put his clothes back on. Glancing at his still naked groin, Xiao Fengxian found the formerly erect sword already lowered. She had wanted to tell him the result of her examination at the hospital and the suggestion of the gynecologist. She wanted to share with him her hope that he would work with her on the treatment, which needed the helping hand of a man. But now he was in a hurry to put his clothes on, looking anxious and eager to get away from her. She felt her heart suddenly drop and a surge of stomach acid shoot up. She didn't want to tell him any more. Judging from the situation, even if she told him, he would not have helped her.

Master Qiu dressed up and said to Xiao Fengxian, who was still lying on the desk: "I've got some business to take care of at home. I'm leaving now." He then opened the office door, and without looking back, stepped out. The door closed behind him. The darkness had deepened outside and yet Xiao Fengxian still lay on the desk. She didn't want to move at all. She wanted to keep lying there. She had no desire to go home. Staring at the dark ceiling, a millions of things ran through her mind. But she still had no idea, no matter how hard she tried, of what had happened and how.

IX

The Funeral Service Corporation had now been in formal existence for a year. As a founding member, Xiao Fengxian was in a position to give instructions and orders. Her principal role was no longer keening but human resources management, a special arrangement by Master Qiu in consideration of her situation. He told her: "Given your physical condition, there is no need for you to be there every time they ask for a keener."

The words of Master Qiu somehow made her feel ill at ease because this was how opera troupes usually eased out an unwanted member, first reducing the number of appearances until there were no appearances at all anymore. So Xiao Fengxian asked him: "What else can I do aside from keening? I am not a composer like you."

Master Qiu replied gently: "All you have to do is to manage the internal affairs of the company and teach your student well. Your salary will not be cut at all. The top priority for you now is to take proper care of yourself."

Xiao Fengxian was touched, her eyes tearing as she answered coquettishly: "So long as you don't kick me out, I'm fine with managing the company affairs and teaching."

Master Qiu remarked disapprovingly: "How could you utter such words? I would never do such a thing. There are so many people working here. Some tried to make a living and some left complaining of poor pay; many come and many go. But you and I, we are always together, rain or shine, in good times and in bad. You can stay so long as the company exists."

These words from Master Qiu cleared up the clog that had been blocking her mind for days, and she felt uplifted. For some time now, because of Master Qiu's refusal to cooperate in treating her hyperplasia problem, Xiao Fengxian had been feeling the blues and her physical condition had also been deteriorating.

Recently she had even fainted while keening at a memorial service. Fortunately, Jiang Meihua was there to be her replacement and did a nice job. But the people in Liuwan still believed in the old brand—however good Jiang Meihua might be, Xiao Fengxian was their preference. They figured that keening was a profession different than that of a singer or movie star. In those businesses, the younger the star, the more drawing power he or she has. But experience in life is a must for a keener; a good voice alone is not enough to make you shine. You need to have reached a certain age and learned enough lessons in life. Compared to Xiao Fengxian, Jiang Meihua was a lightweight, and just that little bit of difference in substance caused their difference in rank. Xiao Fengxian still occupied the number one keener position, unchallenged for the time being.

She didn't take anything for granted, however. In her heart, she always maintained a sense of urgency and alert. She knew full well that life was unpredictable. Whatever was fact in the morning might not hold true by night-time, and you also might not be around to see tomorrow. Of course, this was exacerbated by her worry about her health. Ever since the fainting incident, Master Qiu began to cut down on her appearances, and now they had dwindled so that she only keened for those who specifically asked for her. All other requests were handled by Jiang Meihua.

She realized that her stamina was simply not what it used to be. Plus her chest pain seemed to have worsened, which she held against Master Qiu. Many times she wanted to ask him to stay behind in the office alone with her. Even if it didn't help her condition, it would at least bring some psychological comfort to her. But Master Qiu was always busy talking to customers about funeral arrangements or making notes and composing scores for new music or elegies. Not only did he not have time to spend with Xiao Fengxian alone, he hardly had time to stop by and talk to her.

However busy he was, Master Qiu would never miss any of his trips to the countryside to collect folk music, so strong was his love for art and his determined pursuit of his artistic career. Except that now instead of Xiao Fengxian, he took Jiang Meihua along on these trips. For Xiao Fengxian's physical wellbeing, wasn't it better for her to rest at home?

His only responsibility was to make sure that she was treated fairly and with respect, and this he did. She got the highest pay for the easiest work. In other words, she was receiving special treatment. But this special treatment didn't seem to have nursed her back to health. Xiao Fengxian felt that her body, without the caressing touch of a man, was like a flower without the drench of rain and dewdrops. She felt she was truly that withering flower, fading and shriveling away. Her full hips had narrowed, and the trousers that had been tight before now felt empty. Her fleshy shoulders seemed all protruding bones. And the two masses of her breasts were now increasingly hard and the nodules were getting more and more visible. Without the help of a man she could only try the gynecologist's recommended treatment on her own. But rubbing and playing with her own body proved to be ineffective, as she felt not the least arousal. Human beings are inexplicable creatures. Sometimes things have to be done by a man to a woman; she can't do them herself with the same result.

One day, as she was lying there rubbing her breasts, which were by then hard as stones, she felt moisture in her palms. Upon closer inspection, she noticed that a yellowish sticky fluid was coming out of her nipples. Heavens, this was not the excess milk that had occasionally come out right after the birth of her son. She realized that she had real problems now. The words uttered by Yao Chunfu once again came to her mind: "A woman who slaps a man will have bad luck." At this thought, her body, hard breasts fully exposed, couldn't but shiver in the cold air.

She paid another visit to the village clinic. And

this time, the plump, dark-skinned gynecologist told her: "The clinic doesn't have the equipment. You need to go to East Hospital for an examination."

Xiao Fengxian traveled alone to her examination at East Hospital, located by the Huangpu River and forty kilometers away from the town of Liuwan. And a week later, she went there again to fetch the report. The doctor there asked her crisply: "Conservative therapy or surgery, what is your choice? Given your present condition, there is still hope for a recovery after surgery, but your right breast needs to be removed. Notify your family and prepare the money for hospitalization."

With the hospitalization papers and the diagnosis of "invasive breast cancer" issued by the doctor in her hand, Xiao Fengxian stepped out of the hospital. Her judgment was announced on the slim piece of paper—she now had a ferocious disease. But she didn't look especially traumatized; neither did she seem to find the news especially unacceptable. She looked very calm, as if this was what she had been expecting. The announcement of the doctor finally made her suspended heart tumble back to its place. She had guessed it, this was the disease. Yao Chunfu's curse had come true.

The doctor had advised her to notify her family. She asked herself, whom should she notify, Yao Chunfu or Master Qiu? After thinking it over, she felt it should be Master Qiu. How could she trust someone like Yao Chunfu? All he did for her was exploit her for money and curse her. Once he knew she had this disease, which would eventually deprive him of his source of funds, wouldn't he try everything to lay his hands on all the money she squirreled away? As to Master Qiu, although he was not her husband and couldn't go out of his way to take care of her, he could at least give her advice in addition to showing the concern and sympathy he must have for her.

On her ride back, Xiao Fengxian decided that she would go directly to see Master Qiu in his office as soon as the bus arrived at Liuwan. She would ask for his opinion about the options of surgery and conservative therapy. She would then go home and take out the savings book she had hidden between boards in the attic, get her clothes ready, and go to the hospital.

If she opted for surgery, she would only have one breast, the one on her left. Would a woman with only one breast still be considered a woman? She became depressed at this thought. But this was the card she was dealt, and there was no way around it. And really, she would be lucky if she ended up only missing one breast. After all one could die of the disease too.

Once she had disembarked, she began walking directly toward the embroidery factory. She wanted to speak to Master Qiu, the one man she could count on and confess her feelings to. Only he could give her the confidence to do what she needed to, even if she only saved just one breast and lived on with that void. At that moment, Xiao Fengxian really missed Master Qiu, the only man who deserved a place in her heart.

The warehouse office was in sight. The man she was looking for should be at that familiar place.

On the horizon, late autumn winds had turned the weeds on the edge of the rice paddy yellow and dry. The sparrows flapped their wings, soaring in the sky and then landing on the ground nonchalantly. The setting sun had colored the whole sky dark brown. The surrounding scenery was an exact a reflection of her state of mind: desolation, loneliness and melancholy all intertwined.

She heard the sound of an *erhu* playing from within, the rise and fall of its melodious tune sounding a bit melancholy. It must be Master Qiu. She felt she was not alone in this wretched world after all. At a time when she was almost torn apart by worries, she still had a man who while playing the *erhu* was waiting for her return. Armed with this blissful feeling, she felt she could even face death without regret. Twitches of pain and emotions she couldn't explain tugged at her heart. On the verge of tears, she continued her walk toward the music.

She was just outside the office door, about to push it open, when she heard a man and a woman talking on top of the sound of the *erhu*. The woman said: "Teacher Qiu, how did you come to know so much?" The man replied: "I love to study these things. Keening is also known as elegy. It is indeed a treasure of our folk culture. *Xielu* comes from the *Book of Songs* and was sung at funerals for people from high society. The tune is elegant and expresses a more controlled sense of grief. Just listen to this. I did the composition myself to follow the meaning of the lyrics:

> How soon the sunlight dries
> The dew that on shallot-leaves lies
> Yet the same dew
> Though now 'tis dry
> Tomorrow morn will fall anew
> But when shall mortal men
> If once they die
> Ever return again?

Listening outside, Xiao Fengxian thought it was all a dream. The conversation between the man and the woman, and the singing and the tune of the *erhu* kept drifting out. She wondered about the owner of the female voice. Was it Jiang Meihua? But at the same time, she thought, it was clearly herself. She could see a woman named Xiao Fengxian, led by a man step by step, getting closer and closer to her dream.

X

Xiao Fengxian was not hospitalized; neither did she tell anyone about her examination. She lay down and rested at home alone for three days. During these three days, Yao Chunfu continued his usual routine of spending all his after-work hours playing mahjongg, not paying the least attention to why she was in bed. During these three days, Master Qiu did pay her a visit, but he was accompanied by her student Jiang Meihua. His greeting and words of comfort sounded formal and he did not dare look her in the eyes.

She then asked herself if there was anything or

anyone else that she still cared about in this world. After some hard thinking, she concluded that aside from her son, nothing and no one else in this world could give her the confidence and motivation to fight this ferocious disease alone. Yao Chunfu was discounted as a possible candidate long ago. And now she had a change of heart about the man who had just come to see her, the man she originally thought was trustworthy. A woman many years her junior was now following him everywhere. His eyes became evasive when he looked at her. The comforting words he uttered also sounded hollow. How could he be trusted? Xiao Fengxian finally saw what had been lurking deep inside her, something that she didn't have the courage to confront—despair. It was now totally exposed.

After Master Qiu left with Jiang Meihua, Xiao Fengxian cried for a long time underneath the comforter, until she had almost no tears left in her. After crying, she decided that she would go back to work tomorrow. She would like to be a responsible mother to her son in the best way she knew how, to leave him with sufficient money.

The next day, Xiao Fengxian went back to work as if nothing had happened. She again took charge of the *erhu*, flutes, gongs, drums and small cymbals as she had before, and fulfilled her duty to Jiang Meihua as a teacher by giving her lessons. Jiang Meihua was getting better and better in her keening skills and had taken over all the keening assignments.

Xiao Fengxian's plan was simple and realistic one: she would make as much money as possible. The longer she could work, the better. She could feel now that what she had was an incurable disease. Her whole chest was in pain, probably a sign of what the doctor called metastasis. No human being can escape death. It is bound to happen sooner or later. Instead of spending money on trying to cure something that cannot be cured, she would rather leave the money to her son.

The only thing she couldn't figure out was who was going to keen for her when she died. Was there someone somewhere who was a better keener than Xiao Fengxian? The best carpenter in the world could prepare his own coffin before his death; the best tailor in the world could sew his or her shroud ahead of time. But it would be impossible for the best keener in the world to keen at her own funeral. She became inconsolable at this thought. When she died, there would be no better keener in the world who could provide the wistful and haunting music that would send her to heaven. How deplorable and pitiful!

She wanted to create an elegy for herself because she was not sure how she would be mourned by another. How could the task of writing an elegy in memory of the best keener fall on someone else? During the day, when other members of the company all left for work, she stayed behind and gave it a try. And she also tried singing the words in the evening after she came home from work. After many revisions and repeated practice in private, the creative process finally came to an end. The elegy was finished.

But who should be given the job of singing this elegy? Jiang Meihua? Xiao Fengxian couldn't and wouldn't trust that woman with the job. There really was no suitable person to be found. She herself was the only option. But if she was dead, how could she keen for herself? Physical symptoms were telling her that she was approaching the end of her life, and yet she still couldn't find a suitable candidate. This had become her obsession, something that haunted every moment.

That winter Yao Chunfu's aunt died. He came to the funeral company looking for Xiao Fengxian, and said to her: "Uncle knows that you work for the company, and through me he would like to ask you to handle the funeral. Since we're family, is it possible to get a discount?"

Xiao Fengxian replied: "I'm not the boss, and I don't have a say on things like this."

Yao Chunfu then said: "Can you talk to Boss Qiu and see if he will agree to a discount?"

This man, who had fought with her because of her rumored affair with Master Qiu, was now addressing his rival as Boss Qiu just for the sake of a discount? Keeping her derisive smile to herself,

Xiao Fengxian said to him: "Why don't you discuss it with him yourself. All I can offer is to keen for your aunt for free."

After thinking about it, Yao Chunfu realized he felt too uncomfortable to see Master Qiu himself. He finally said: "Fine, fine. You be the keener and waive the fee for the sake of my uncle. For everything else we'll just follow the rules."

Xiao Fengxian had not keened for others for quite a while, but she was determined to do it herself this time. In her dual role as the wife of the nephew of the deceased and the company keener, she arrived together with the band and other people at the funeral location in a village outside town.

Once they went inside the yard, Master Qiu busied himself giving out assignments, making sure that the decorations were properly done, and checking that everyone was in position. He also needed to tell the host what to do. Today's funeral was no different from a large assembly, with complicated requirements for procedures and ceremonies. Master Qiu not only needed to direct his own people but also the relatives of the deceased family, so he needed to enlist their cooperation. With all of this, Master Qiu had been kept busy ever since he set foot on the scene.

Clad in white funeral clothes with a white band around her waist, Xiao Fengxian sat silently in a corner of the memorial hall, waiting for the funeral to begin. Usually the professional keener is not required to wear white, but today she was also a relative. As a member of the next generation of the deceased's family, she was pulled to the side and wrapped with a white cloth around her waist the minute she stepped in. She let the women dress her without any protest.

After they were done, she sat down and looked around. On one side of the hall, the deceased lay in a bed placed in a corner underneath a white sheet piled with plastic flowers. The walls were covered with colorful memorial couplets on silk, and the air was filled with the smoke of candles and incense. The female relatives were chatting cheerfully while folding ritual paper money for the deceased. It actually looked more like a feast than a funeral occasion. Since the deceased lived to a ripe old age, it was natural that people didn't feel that bereft. Funerals such as this were often referred to as "happy funerals."

Under a tent in the large yard outside were dozens of tables that could accommodate eight people. After the conclusion of the service they would be used for serving a traditional tofu banquet to the guests. Seats around seven or eight tables were already taken. The sound of mahjongg being played and the noise of the crowd made it a lively scene.

This was the custom of the villages surrounding Liuwan; in the event of a death, the whole village would turn out to help. The deceased had to stay home for three days before the funeral, and the sons and daughters and their spouses were all supposed to join the wake. So if they were all occupied, who would be in charge of the tofu banquet? Who would buy the white cloth to make flowers and the black cloth for mourning bands? All these tasks were done by the neighbors. In return, the host needed to show them hospitality, feeding them well and letting them play mahjongg and cards outside the hall.

For people usually caught up in their own affairs, deaths provided rare opportunities for them to get together and enjoy each other's company. The comings and goings of these people over the three days were meant to liven up the atmosphere, which would otherwise seem overly forlorn and forsaken. When there was a death in the family, this was the way to go: the mingling of the sounds of mourning, chatting and mahjongg playing conveyed a sense of prosperity.

Looking around, Xiao Fengxian immediately recognized the slim figure of her husband Yao Chunfu. He was among the tables of mahjongg players. His hands were busy drawing and discarding tiles. Bills—small and large—were laid out nearby. His eyes were red from lack of sleep. It was obvious to her that he had been playing almost non-stop for three days, although those who didn't know him might get the mistaken impression that his eyes were red from crying for his aunt. At this sight, the question that came to her mind was: "When my time comes, will Yao Chunfu also behave like this, taking his place at the mahjongg table?" This thought left her feeling lost and empty and immensely sad. Flustered, she could also feel the pain in her chest hitting her in waves, as if on cue.

The service finally started just before noon. With the arrival of the first batch of guests, Xiao Fengxian put her mind to her keening, and she continued on, addressing the different groups. When it was the sons' turn to dress the deceased, she sang the "dressing song" and when it was the daughters-in-law's turn to comb the hair of their mother-in-law, she keened the "combing song." Her plaintive and touching rendering reduced all the female relatives, who moments ago were folding paper money while happily chitchatting with each other, to tears. The crowd watching on the side was unanimous in their praise, giving her their approval: the number one keener is indeed different. Her mastery of the art was apparent the minute she opened her mouth.

By the time the funeral procession started, Xiao

Fengxian had cried her throat dry and was exhausted. The body of the deceased was carried to the hall entrance. The back door of the hearse provided by the funeral company was kept open in the courtyard, waiting for the body to enter its black hole. Carried on both sides by two women, Xiao Fengxian walked in faltering steps toward the hearse, and then knelt down behind the family of the deceased. Keening had left her extremely thirsty and she had a sharp pain in her chest. She wanted some water and to sit down and rest.

She raised her head to search for someone with a cup of water but saw only the faces of strangers and piles of colorful wreaths. Only two tables of mahjongg players out of the seven or eight were still at the game under the oil-cloth tent, and her husband was sitting in the same place, feeling the tiles in his hand, his head lowered, not even bothering to lift his eyelids.

As another wave of chest pain shot up she almost fell to the ground. Her mind went blank but her ears could still hear the familiar tunes of the funeral music, every note and every passage of which she knew by heart. And what about the man who conducted this music? She looked in the direction of the ensemble located at the other end of the yard, and saw a shiny head bobbing energetically with the music. The man, immersed in the music of his own creation, was enjoying the satisfaction and sense of accomplishment brought on by the music that mourned the dead. As she listened, the music seemed so intimate and so close, as if it was played for her own funeral. In her mind's eye she could visualize a memorial service held at a later time, with the man's bald head bobbing, and beautiful funeral music being played for a dead woman called Xiao Fengxian.

As the family members of the deceased who were kneeling in rows ahead of Xiao Fengxian emitted an enormous howl, the time for the most solemn procession was at hand. As the howling died down, the scene was enveloped in total silence, and everyone awaited her final keening performance, the piece-de-resistance of the whole funeral. Xiao Fengxian raised her head and scanned her surroundings, the audience's expressions of anticipation flashing in her mind. She became confused. Where was she? Was she at a long-ago performance? Were these people waiting for her to sing her famous rendition of "Baoyu by the Bier"?

No, no. She had long ago stopped being the performing artist who sang that piece. She was now a keener, participating in a funeral, and she was about to keen for a dead soul. And that dead person was herself. She was at her own funeral, keening for none other than Xiao Fengxian.

The elegy she created for herself suddenly came to her mind, the elegy she had written for her own funeral and for which she had so far failed to find a suitable keener. Now the words and the phrases appeared in her head, ready to float out in words and song as soon as she opened her mouth. She didn't care whether the elegy fit the occasion of this funeral, nor did she care if there would be objections to its lyrics. She opened her mouth, and people heard this piercing cry: "My dear relative! I call you again, my dear relative, I will walk with you..."

Everyone felt shaken to the bone by this initial cry. Goose bumps crept up their skin. The words of the elegy sung by Xiao Fengxian, the indisputable number one keener of Liuwan, slowly advanced:

I call you again, my dear relative,
Let me walk with you.
On your journey alone,
You need to watch out for dangers unknown.
Looks can be deceiving,
Dogs may block your road to the underworld.

Capable as you were, fate was not with you.
When fate went against you, life was hard;
Illness and misfortunes were the least of worries,
What hurt the most was when your heart broke apart.
Strong as you were, fate was not with you.
When fate went against you, no one was there to love you,
And care for you except yourself, all your life,

Toward paradise you strive.

I call you again, my dear relative,

Let me walk with you one more time.

As you cross roads and bridges,

Never step back and return.

Never return to the life of bitterness,

As bitter as it tastes,

when the bile duct of the carp is pierced by a needle.

Even reincarnated as a blade of grass,

Life would be better than the wretched one you had;

Drenched with morning dew and warmed by sunshine,

The grass could never be condemned or cursed.

Even reincarnated as a duck,

Life would be better than the wretched one you had;

Swimming in the water and chasing after fish,

Quacking happily when you are cared for and fed.

I call you again, my dear relative,
Let me walk with you one last time.
On your way to the Nine Springs,
You will be alone for the last leg.
Walk with steady steps,
Stop and rest and mind your surroundings.

The sky is dark, and so is the ground,
The road is bumpy, not easily found;
Let me light a lamp for you,
So you won't trip or be scared,
By the silence and cold;
Let me sing a song for you,
So you will be emboldened to continue.

My dear relative! I call you, my dear relative!
Take another look at me,
Respond to me one more time.
My dear relative, take good care!

The beautiful rendering of the elegy floated far

and wide in the nipping cold air of the beginning of spring. The soul of the dead was leaving the battered body and flying into the remote distance. Through her teary eyes Xiao Fengxian seemed to have seen the world hidden at the far end of the sky. It was a world where the weather was forever mild and pleasant, and the flowers in constant bloom. A world where there was no opera piece entitled "Baoyu by the Bier," no death, and certainly no keener to cry for the dead.

Stories by Contemporary Writers from Shanghai

The Little Restaurant
Wang Anyi

A Pair of Jade Frogs
Ye Xin

Forty Roses
Sun Yong

Goodby, Xu Hu!
Zhao Changtian

Vicissitudes of Life
Wang Xiaoying

The Elephant
Chen Cun

Folk Song
Li Xiao

The Messenger's Letter
Sun Ganlu

Ah, Blue Bird
Lu Xing'er

His One and Only
Wang Xiaoyu

When a Baby Is Born
Cheng Naishan

Dissipation
Tang Ying

Paradise on Earth
Zhu Lin

The Most Beautiful Face in the World
Xue Shu

Beautiful Days
Teng Xiaolan